Pieces of BLUE

USA Today Bestselling Author

LIZ FLAHERTY

Pieces of Blue by Liz Flaherty
Published by Singing Tree Publishing

Previously published by Annessa Ink

“Look for the helpers.” - Fred Rogers

I can’t begin to count the helpers I’ve known in my life, and it is to them this book is dedicated, with admiration and gratitude.

TABLE OF CONTENTS

Chapter 1

Trilby died.

I'm Maggie North. That has been my name for most of my adult life, with a few years out for being an idiot, but the day of Trilby Winterroad's death became the center pole on my lifeline. Not when I graduated, married, was widowed or, later, divorced after a disastrous second marriage that comprised the idiot years. I measured my life from the cold day in early February when Trilby died and what came after.

We pieced together his last day after bidding him farewell in a quiet, private service and following the hearse to the little family cemetery on a hillside in central Michigan where he was buried beside the woman he'd been married to for fifty years. Beautiful, excruciatingly shy Claire had died a few years earlier, her body unable to beat a recurrence of cancer. Trilby had never known a day of contentment, much less happiness, since.

He spent the morning with Sam, his lawyer, got several notes in his leggy handwriting notarized, and left a hundred-dollar tip with his favorite barista at the coffee shop. He left a blue binder full of notes for his next book on my desk, laid printed funeral instructions on his own, then took a cocktail of drugs he'd researched when he wrote *Mayhem in the Cascades.* While he was still conscious, he called the pastor of the Episcopal Church, his sons, and me. By the time he called the EMTs to prevent any of us from being the ones to find him, he sounded sleepy and urged them not to hurry.

Then, dressed in the jeans and sweatshirt he wore almost every day, he lay on the couch in his office with his longhaired dachshund Chloe curled up beside him and died.

He chose a day I wasn't at work. I'd taken it off to celebrate a clear mammogram with my best friend and nurse practitioner, Ellie Wentz. I know it's unreasonable, but I've found it difficult to forgive myself for that. How could I not have known?

Back in Muskegon in my apartment after the funeral, I made coffee for Trilby's two sons and their wives, the lawyer, agent, and housekeeper who were with him nearly as long as I was.

"He called us that morning," said his eldest son Tom's wife, Miriam. "That should have been a clue. There hasn't been a Winterroad born yet who talks on the phone before coffee."

"He told me I was the best birthday present he ever had." Josie was married to Dan, his second son. Her voice failed, and she swallowed hard enough for me to see the movement in her throat and went on. "He always told me that, but then he'd say '*But who likes birthday presents?*' and we'd both laugh like it was a new joke."

"He paid me in cash," said Ruby, the housekeeper. "He never did that before, and his note said he was giving me my birthday and Christmas bonuses early." Her eyes were red from weeping. "How could I not have known?"

"I'm certain he didn't mean for anyone to know." Sam Eldridge, whom Trilby had subsidized through law school, spoke quietly. "He got every duck in a row. If there are things with the placement of said ducks that any of you don't agree with, feel free to take it up with me." His smile was faint. "Since, as far as I know, you're all my clients, I'm afraid the only one who would benefit from that would be me."

"Is this the official reading of the will then?" asked Tom. "Where one of us stands up and bellows that we'll contest it?"

"It is." Sam handed out copies of the document. "As you know, the grandchildren all have trust funds—enough for college but not if they drink too much beer while they're there. He also had bequests for them that have already been taken care of. They can't be touched for quite some time. Trilby had a touch of the control freak in him."

The comment drew laughter, the relieving kind that often comes in the middle of profound grief. “Just a touch,” agreed Dan. “I was actually born first, but since Pop liked Tom better, he let him be the oldest.”

“I didn’t realize you knew,” Tom said in a scandalized stage whisper. “Who *told* you?”

The brothers, both perfect combinations of their parents, laughed again, and we laughed with them. We were all Trilby’s family. We grieved, but laughter had been a mainstay all of his life—he wouldn’t be happy if we stopped now.

We skimmed the copies of the will, the reading glasses that decorated our faces attesting to our age group. Its contents were written in sparse language, leaving no room for argument or ambiguity.

“I am disappointed.” Laughter still lingered in Tom’s voice, lightening the heaviness that threatened the atmosphere in the apartment. “Not a word about the legendary sapphires that came to America with our Australian great-grandparents sewed into…something. I don’t remember what, do you, Danny?”

Dan shook his head. “No. The story changed every time he told it.”

I kept looking for mention of Greg Mathis, Trilby’s adopted brother and my ex-husband, but there was none. Not even the proverbial dollar. He was still in prison as far as I knew. I had no idea if he’d even been informed of Trilby’s death. I certainly wasn’t going to be the one to tell him. Other than a gasp from Ruby, no one said anything until Miriam said, "It's wonderfully generous and more than fair."

Everyone murmured agreement except me—I was surprised into silence. I knew, of course, that there would be special instructions concerning me, but figured they'd all have to do with business.

Nothing had prepared me to inherit a house I didn't know existed on a lake I've never heard of. As with the other bequests, a note was included. *I'm not going to insist you go to Harper Loch to live—insisting never works with you anyway. But it's time to live your own life, find your own voice. Remember there's always a treasure out there. Look to the sun, Margaret Mary. That's where you'll find it. For better or worse. – TW*

~*~*~

I spent the next two weeks clearing out Trilby's office and helping his family prepare his condo for sale. Although a part of me was angry with him for ending his own life, I was grateful for how he'd left things. Other than the sapphires Tom and Dan thought were probably figments of their father's fertile imagination, very few t's had been left uncrossed or i's undotted.

I have no doubt he understood the sense of disconnection his death would leave me with. I worked for him for thirty-six years, starting when I was sixteen. Other than Ellie, my best friend since second grade, I no longer had a sense of anchorage in Muskegon. There was no one left to miss. Even Sam, who'd been my *what happens now?* person often enough that I occasionally think I should keep him on retainer, was a professional acquaintance.

No, that's wrong. If I'm honest about it, he's probably my best friend after Ellie. There has been more than one flicker of … something … between us in the years of that friendship, but first he was married and then I was. Then he wasn't and I was again. Nothing made us think pursuing a flicker would be a good idea. While we saw each other socially sometimes, it was usually in the company of others.

I was even able to disregard the fact that Sam's looks had a whole lot in common with those of a fifty-some Mark Harmon. Usually.

The condo where Trilby and I had worked was completely cleared of any evidence we'd ever been there. Painters had come in and painted the walls ubiquitous white. The floors had been cleaned. It would sell, the realtor assured Tom and Dan, within days.

I sat across from Ellie at the Black Dog, the coffee house that had crossed to the wild side and served beer and wine. It had only been days since my life had changed entirely, I reminded myself, staring into the glass of merlot. "Do you think Scott just puts red food coloring in this and passes it off for wine?"

Ellie shrugged. "Hey, three bucks a glass. Who's gonna complain?"

"Good point." I scooted the glass aside and looked down at the notes I'd taken on Harper Loch. "All I can find out is that the lake covers forty-some acres. It has a population of somewhere between 85 and 212 depending on the time of year, and you can buy milk, bread, and beer at the combination store and bait shop. The store's name is Harper Mercantile. Placer, the closest town with any real amenities, is five miles away. It has two stoplights plus a caution light at the junction where the main street meets the highway. There's a library, a doctor, a quilt shop, a vet, and an ice cream shop. Oh, and a boutique and at least one café. I'm sure there's more, but that was sufficient unto my needs, so I stopped reading."

"So, what are you going to do?" Ellie looked at me, concern on her face. "I know you can stay busy doing the promotion for Trilby's books and giving talks at bookstores and libraries about what it was like being his assistant, but I don't see that being enough for you."

"I'll finish the one I'm working on and I have his notes for another. After that, I'm not sure."

"More Lunchroom Mysteries?"

"No. We stopped those when the kids aged out." I tilted up the glass, drained it, and refilled it from the bottle we shared. I was glad I brought an Uber to Black Dog. Food coloring or not, I was a little … foggy.

"What if you go to this lake in the middle of nowhere and decide you like it there?"

I snorted. I'd never lived outside city limits in my life. "Like that's going to happen. But Tom and Dan asked if I'd like to have Chloe, Trilby's dog, since she knew me better than anyone else because I saw her every day. I talked to her about it and she's all for going to the lake for a few days—maybe even a few weeks. I need a break from Muskegon and she needs to stop looking for Trilby."

"Makes sense to me." Ellie looked a little sad, probably more a product of the wine than the conversation. At least, I hoped it was.

"He never mentioned this lake to you?"

I'd already answered that more than once to more than one person, and I tried to remember every time. "No, but I've said it so often I'm not sure anymore. It's only about two hours from where he and Claire lived—but farther north and east."

"How did he end up in Muskegon? He grew up out east, didn't he?"

I shook my head. "He grew up on the farm where he and Claire lived. He went to the University of Michigan. They lived in Muskegon when they were first married because he taught at the community college, but when his wife moved to the farm with the kids to care for her mother, she stayed there. It reminded her of where she grew up in France. They sold their house and boat in Muskegon and bought the condo where he worked and stayed Monday through Thursday. He went home every weekend."

"I knew he did." Ellie shrugged. "It just seems weird."

"Not so much." At least, I didn't think it did. "His whole life was his family and writing books and Muskegon—he loved it here and even when he changed to adjunct status, he continued teaching at the college. He had no social life that I know of outside of those. Trilby and Claire were intensely private, and it was what worked for them." I straightened in my chair. "I've just talked about his life more than I did all the years I worked for him. This food coloring is making me share a little too much."

"It's safe with me. I liked Trilby and Claire." Ellie made a salami, cracker, and cheese sandwich from the charcuterie board between us. "Want me to go with you to the lake?"

"Not this time. Let this just be the fact-finding tour. I may want to do no more than look at it and list it. My life is here."

As soon as the words left my mouth, I wished they hadn't. The weight of grief they unloaded was crushing.

What life?

"Is it?" said Ellie, handing me a sandwich like the one she'd made herself. "Are you content with it?"

"To use the words Trilby hated more than any other, it is what it is." *And it's nothing. Other women draw life and identity from being mothers, wives, successful in their life's work. Not me. My whole life and identity are wrapped up in being Trilby Winterroad's assistant and ghost writer.*

That life was over, ended by Trilby's final act. Or would be soon. I had one book to finish and another to write.

How could you?

It wasn't the first time I'd thought that, or the question's partner—*Why did you?*

I left soon, congratulating the Uber driver on his new baby and leaving a bigger tip than I normally would have because seeing his little girl's picture was a great reminder of the presence of joy. I took the elevator to my apartment in a building that had a harbor view if I stood on one side of the balcony and leaned almost far enough to the right to fall over the rail. I was tired and more depressed than I cared to admit. Chloe met me at the door, asking politely for a walk.

I kept my coat on and fastened the dog's leash to her collar. "I'm not used to you, am I, girl?" I'd never had a pet before and while I was charmed by Chloe, I was occasionally irritated by the responsibility.

I packed for the drive to Harper Loch the following morning, not certain what to take or how long I'd be there. It was only about two hours away … or maybe three; it was a crooked route. When Sam called to assure me the lock code was up-to-date, he told me the house was live-in ready, with utilities already on. "Don't come back right away," he urged. "Give yourself some time. Trilby left things well taken care of."

Driving out of Muskegon with Chloe in the passenger seat and an audiobook playing, I laughed at myself for being a little excited, but I'd never traveled for my own purposes—although I wasn't sure a three-hour drive within my own state qualified. When Tim, my first husband and the love of my life, was ill, we made the drive to Ann Arbor for doctor's appointments and treatment several times a week. We used to say our worst days were also our best ones. We'd talked all the way there and back, and when Tim was too ill to do his part, I talked for both of us, sometimes arriving home hoarse.

Twenty-five years after his death, I still missed him. "He was the nicest guy ever born," I told Chloe. "We laughed so much. When he was gone, I thought I'd never laugh again."

I'm not sure I have yet, either. Well, I've laughed. I was even happy for a while when Trilby introduced me to Greg and I married him too quickly. It was the single most impetuous thing I've ever done. And the most foolish.

"How about you, Chloe? Were you married before Trilby rescued you? Was it a mistake?" I didn't remember laughing aloud in a car by myself before, but the idea that I was carrying on a conversation with a dog tickled me.

Other than the trip to the cemetery for Trilby's burial, it had been a few years since I'd been very far into Michigan's interior. I'd had no reason after Claire's death. I'd forgotten how pretty it was, even in February. The roads were clear after I left the highway, but the fields and woods were snow-covered. What had looked like a maybe-three-hour drive on the map had extended into nearly four after two stops to walk Choe.

The town of Placer was bigger than I had expected. When I took a wrong turn because I was gaping at all the trees in the town, I found myself in front of a brick Victorian house that declared itself to be JOSETTA'S QUILT SHOP. The sign on its oversized front door invited me to COME IN, so I did. In the second room of the shop, I saw a quilt draped gracefully over a balustrade somewhere above my head and stopped to stare at it.

It took my breath away. Aunt Lin, who'd made quilts for as long as I could remember, would have been in ecstasy, and I wasn't far behind that. I pointed at it. "For sale?"

The colors were mesmerizing, especially the blues, in what the Amish woman making the sale told me was the *Be My Neighbor* pattern. The quilt would in no way go with the muted grays and soft whites of my apartment, but I didn't care. I didn't think I'd ever bought anything simply because it was beautiful. Maybe it was time.

"You may like it from afar," I told Chloe when I got back in the car, "but it's a people quilt."

Although the lake was within five miles of Placer, the drive took me deeper into the country than I'd ever been—at least that I could remember. While the temperature didn't drop, the wind did increase, blowing snow from the roadsides across in front of me in gusty swirls of white. I was surprised that Gladys, the elegant voice of my GPS, didn't sound either confused or disdainful even when it took me three tries to see the little green sign that indicated HARPER LOCH ROAD.

Canopied by naked February trees and lined with animal-tracked snowbanks, the road was one and a half lanes wide. I hoped it would be wider when there was no snow, but I wouldn't bet on it. It was hilly, with serpentine curves that reminded me of a Chutes and Ladders game board minus the ladders. Gladys didn't enlighten me as to how far it was to the lake itself, and two miles in, I was starting to wonder if it was all a bad joke.

Trilby had been the master of bad jokes, the way he died being the worst one of all.

A barnwood sign at the side of the road encouraged me to *KEEP RIGHT!* I inched over, flinching when the snowbank brushed the side of my car, my pride and joy. Chloe looked my way, wide-eyed.

Apparently, it was a popular meeting spot on the road, because a pickup popped over the slight hill immediately, going at least twice as fast as I was. The driver waved cheerfully and missed me by what I was certain was the hair's breadth Trilby used to insist was purple prose if used in a book. I would have waved back, but my hands, white knuckled, didn't want to let go of the steering wheel.

"Trilby," I said, "what in the hell were you thinking?"

Chapter 2

I was still breathing hard when I crested the hill, Chloe accompanying me with little gasps. I should have been on foot, carrying a walking stick and a backpack and singing about the hills being alive. Chloe should have been standing triumphantly in the breeze with her ears blowing back from her wise little face. But we were still in the car, coasting gently down the hill toward the cluster of houses in the woods that surrounded a flat expanse of the lake. "We're fine," I assured her, not sure at all that I was being truthful. Could one go to hell for lying to a dog?

There it was. If I hadn't known it already, the sign that bid me WELCOME TO HARPER LOCH. SPEED LIMIT 20. POPULATION: VARIES.

I'd arrived at Harper Loch without any perception of how big forty acres was. Not even a little bit. I've seen Lake Michigan most every day of my life, for God's sake—how could I be impressed by a body of water too small to support speed boats? Maybe *impressed* wasn't the right word.

I just liked it.

According to the directions in Sam's shockingly neat handwriting, I was supposed to follow the road—the name of which had at some point changed to ENOCH

TRACE—until I saw a large rural mailbox with a sign on its post proclaiming the property to be THE BURL. In the trees, up a slight rise—this part of Michigan seemed to be full of "slight rises"—would be the house. It was called the Burl, I was told in the directions, because it had been built and added onto in fits and starts so that its layout was as twisted and whimsical as the burl of an old tree.

The paved driveway had been cleared of snow. It curved gracefully around to the back of the house. A three-car garage sat at an odd angle from the two-story residence. At least, it was two stories in the middle and off in at least one direction. Some of its embellishments were only one level, but there was a tower that looked as if it might be three. The house reminded me of the actress who'd played Mammy in *Gone with the Wind.* Big and curvy (even if the house's curves angled instead of flowed) and strong. Built to protect and give love where it was needed. I knew the thought was whimsical. It was also accurate.

Dark brown wood siding covered both the house and the garage, relieved by the buttercup yellow of the doors. The yellow looked like sunshine.

I'd never had a house. Trilby had suggested it a few times when I'd complained about my rent going up. "It would be an investment like your condo was."

But it wouldn't be like the condo was. A house would end up being important, a safe place, a reflection of who I am. Selling the condo had been easy—I bought the foreclosed unit near Trilby's because a healthy tax refund burned a hole in the pocket of the sweater I wore at work. I'd never made it a part of me and it had ended up being the most unsafe place I'd ever known. It had meant no more to me than the apartment where I lived now; a house would be different.

I remember thinking I'd never be able to make Trilby understand that I needed things to be easy. Many people bounce back readily from things that knock them down. I'm not one of those people.

But he had apparently understood very well.

Outside the car, Chloe took a reluctant trot through the snow to lay claim to the trunk of a white cedar tree that stood sentry over a large shed while I pressed the digits on the back door lock. I left my luggage in the conveniently hooked and shelved mudroom, poked my head into a laundry room that was as big as my apartment's living room, and went into the kitchen.

I liked to cook, but it was only fun if there were people to cook *for*. I was here with eighty-five people I didn't know and Chloe had a delicate constitution—cooking much for these few days here to check out the place was silly.

But … oh, this kitchen …

I walked around looking at waxed floorboards scattered with old-fashioned rag rugs, beamed beadboard ceilings, and a bank of glistening windows over the counter where a double sink was. The appliances were black. Not new, I didn't think, but not that old, either. The cabinets were a mixture of colors and textures. Sage green butted up against a kind of wood I couldn't identify. Blue accents were everywhere, including a few cupboards and in the transoms over the bank of windows.

The windows.

There are no words to explain how much I love all the shades that gather under blue's color umbrella. They made me think of the mythical Winterroad family sapphires. I'm just loaded with whimsey today.

At the end of the long room, a coffee bar and a table and four chairs sat in a large alcove with French doors opening onto a deck.

"Wow," I said. I just kept looking. Why had this lake, this house, this *kitchen* been such a secret?

A whimper from the back door drew my attention, and I let Chloe into the house. "Let's go look."

The Burl was fully furnished, albeit sparsely and not always how I would choose, other than the gorgeous studio piano that sat in a roomy bay at one end of the living room. The house boasted several such spaces, where intimacy could be found. The piano was warmly, deliciously in tune, and I didn't want to leave its sturdy bench when I sat down to wander through a medley of Cole Porter songs. I played until my fingers hurt so much they'd barely move. In the corner of the alcove, a guitar leaned into a stand. I looked at the natural-wood Guild as I played. Thinking it looked familiar. Wondering who played these instruments—or who had.

The floors were all wood except for the bathrooms, windows all open to light but with privacy slats at the top of each one, ready to draw down. The house was warm and I had no idea yet where the heat came from, but there was a fireplace in the living room and wood stacked neatly in a wrought-iron rack near it. A fire was laid. That charmed me somehow. It was so … movieish.

The five rooms upstairs had beds with headboards all different from each other and what looked like new mattresses. I'd never seen so many closets in one place, and reflected I could get everything I owned into one of them and still have room left over. The big downstairs bedroom had been added on facing the lake. Its bathroom had a round window of leaded glass. I stood transfixed by it. It had more blue in it than most of the others. Its panes reminded me of a pie, including the curly wood trim around the outside.

I ached with love, unexpected and rich. I hadn't yet seen the house in its entirety and I already dreaded leaving it.

The office opened off the same short hall as the bedroom. The room was fully equipped, furnished with an old teacher's desk I recognized as having belonged to Trilby. A typewriter table that matched it held a printer and a fax machine. Not everyone uses them anymore, but I still love their immediacy. He had gotten the office furniture from the college when his desk was replaced with a modern unit, I assumed he'd taken them to the farm, but apparently he hadn't.

He'd obviously had this wonderful secret place for a while.

Another transomed window looked onto the front yard with its assortment of trees and what looked like a rose arbor. The lake lay beyond, calm and beautiful. The room was one I could work in. I tried dismissing the notion, but it stayed in the cluttered place that held most of my thoughts these days.

I wondered what color the roses would be.

Blue showed up in unexpected places. A couple of bottles on the mantel, a quilt on the back of the couch, and jeweled pulls on the shades. Accent walls, particularly in the rooms that weren't strictly rectangular or square varied from cool turquoise to deep navy.

The odd spaces captivated me. A room that reminded me of a roundabout was a library, complete with rolling ladder and lovely curved shelves between the doorways that led to different areas in the house.

Transoms appeared over some of the doorways and at the top of several large windows, a few with clear leaded glass and others with the shimmering colors that made me think of cocktail rings on gnarled fingers—a leftover of some of Trilby's earliest mysteries.

I put my things away in the downstairs bedroom, reflecting to Chloe that stopping at a grocery store on the way to the lake might have been a good consideration. "I didn't know if we'd be staying, but I think we will. At least for a day or two. That okay with you?"

Two dog dishes were under the sink. Of course they were. Didn't everyone keep dog bowls just in case a perfect stranger showed up with an adopted dog in tow? When I used the bathroom, I found the kind of toilet paper I buy, the scent of soap I use. Towels in soft coral, jade, and a shade of blue that was quieter than royal or cobalt. Warmer.

I felt the slightest bit creeped out. I mean, who knew about my fondness for that branch of brightness on the blue tree? Who knew I loved creamy liquid soap scented with lavender and sage? I was an alone person who didn't share all that much about myself. My Facebook photo was a sprig of lavender, but that wouldn't be very informative to the most curious of trolls, I wouldn't think. Ellie might have known those things, but she wouldn't have entered into a conversation about them. If Tim had lived, he'd have known.

Wondering if the mercantile had more than just the items I'd read about on the internet when I looked up Harper Loch, I got back into my coat and boots. Chloe offered a baleful look in response to my invitation for her to join me, so I folded a shopping bag into my pocket and put on gloves and the knitted hat my aunt had sent me. "I'll be back. If I'm not here by dark, call someone."

It wasn't yet four o'clock, but darkness hung heavy in the sky. The breeze off the water was cold, smacking damply against my cheeks. Gloominess was a study in black and white and gray, accentuated by the bare trees and unrelieved snow. Lights shone through windows of most of the thirty-some houses around the lake, although some of them were stark in their darkness. They looked lonely. The occasional old-fashioned street lamp shone purplish blue on the snow.

The group of houses was like a microcosm of the small towns in every cozy mystery ever written. The lots appeared to be different sizes, and snow precluded being able to tell how well kept the yards were. I liked nice yards. I liked gardens. I liked flowers.

At least I liked them in magazines. I guess I'd never had them in real life. The duplexes in my aunt and uncle's neighborhood had been so close to the ones next door that their front and back yards had been taken up by sidewalks and carports. The apartment I shared with Tim had been small and sweet. We'd saved faithfully to buy a house, but after he died, I had no heart left for it. I let the dream go and spent our savings on the funeral. That's how you get through things. You let them go—or so I've heard.

Harper Loch didn't boast sidewalks. When you walked there, you either took the path on the shore of the lake or stayed on the narrow road that circled the water.

Some of the houses were shabby, although they looked sturdy. Several mobile homes were on lots in a second row, as if they were just barely respectable. On the other side of the lake, a large white house backed into the woods just as Burl did on my side.

My side? Get a grip, Maggie.

The mercantile was at the end of the lake where the public access was, and it offered a lot more than bait, milk, and bread. Compared to a supersize market, I guess it wasn't much, but as a neighborhood grocery, it was well-stocked, well-lit, and very, very clean. I was charmed yet again.

"You the lady that owns the Burl now?" asked the young man in the deli section who bagged the turkey wrap and macaroni salad that were going to be my dinner.

I nodded. "For now, anyway."

"It's a nice house. Mrs. Newland was a nice lady, too."

The back of my neck prickled. Trilby had released twenty children's books, the Lunchroom Mysteries, under the name Paris Newland. "Mrs. Newland?"

"Yeah, the lady who lived there before. She died back in the fall."

"Do you know her first name?"

"No, but she was French-Canadian. Us kids used to ask her to speak French for us, because it was so pretty."

"I'll bet it was." Trilby had loved the language. He'd met Claire in France, and they went back at least once a year until her mother came to live with them. The name *Paris* had been a nod to Claire. I wondered now if the previous owner of the big house on the little lake had something to do with *Newland.*

The young clerk gestured at the groceries I'd placed in one of the five little carts from the front of the store. "Are you walking, ma'am? If you are, I can drop those off for you. It'll only take a minute to run them over and leave them on the back porch. I used to put them in the mudroom for Mrs. Newland."

I estimated the size of my grocery order, decided that carrying it the remaining distance around the lake wasn't viable, and said, "That would be very kind. The back door is locked, though." And I wasn't going to share its code with a young man I didn't know, no matter how blue his eyes were behind the glasses he wore.

"That's okay. I'll leave it on the table on the deck in one of the foam coolers we have for bait." He grinned. "I'll use a new one, I promise—it won't smell a bit like bait."

"Then thank you very much." I sound awkward to myself. I'm not used to people doing things for me, regardless of having just inherited a house and all its contents. "I'm Maggie North. May I ask your name?"

"Eamon Squires." He waved an arm in a vague direction. "We live in the yellow house down that way. The Bee."

"Well, thank you."

Coffee and tall to-go cups were offered up front, and I bought one to take with me on my walk around the lake. I left a tip for young Eamon with the cashier. "Be safe," she said, smiling. "The icc under that snow will get you in a heartbeat."

I knew that, although I'd been able to avoid the elements in Muskegon. On days the weather turned nasty, I worked from home. I'd liked doing that, although it was disturbing sometimes when I had to clear my throat before speaking because I hadn't used my voice since sometime the previous day.

The sky had darkened more still while I was in the store. It was February in Michigan, after all—what did I expect? I hadn't checked the weather. Had that been foolish?

Most of the houses were pretty, even the ones that needed paint or repair. Names of many of them were burned into barnwood signs that hung on gates or porch railings or occasionally under the front porch light. The Burl was one of the nicer homes here, and easily one of the biggest. That gave me a weird feeling, like the writer friends with imposter syndrome that Trilby used to talk about. How did I end up with a house several times as big as anywhere I'd ever lived? What was I going to *do* with a house that big?

A woman was getting mail from the rural box at the end of her driveway when I trudged past. She waved and I waved back, suddenly missing Ellie and the little gaggle of classmates from my Muskegon High School class who were still my best friends. Except for Ellie, I didn't see them often, but they were my touchstone, I think—my grasp on reality. They would love the Burl.

Not that I'm removed from reality, but I do address it on my own terms.

I slowed, squinting to read yet another barnwood sign in front of a periwinkle cottage trimmed in sage green whose attached garage was bigger than it was. There must have been an awfully big barn somewhere that had come down to create all these signs. This one proclaimed the pretty house to be LAVENDER PARK, with SALON underneath in smaller curling letters. I thought of my shoulder-length wavy hair and thought I should do something with it. Tim used to call it whiskey-colored, but I thought it looked more like soybeans gone dry in the fields. The silver strands that were the consistency of the first string on a guitar did little to alleviate that impression.

By the time I got back to the Burl, the cooler was on the back porch. Chloe was waiting when I stepped sock-footed into the kitchen. Her eyes were bright and curious. "If you'd gone with me," I told her, putting items into the refrigerator and slipping her a piece of deli ham in the process, "you'd know what was going on. You'll like Eamon, I'll bet, if we stay."

What did I mean, *If we stay?* I wasn't going to be a country girl at this stage of my life. Muskegon wasn't particularly large, but it had all the conveniences I liked. I went weeks on end without driving my car any farther than to Trilby's condo or to Tom's Market for groceries. I felt safe where I lived, certain of both police protection and the security in my building. The hospital was minutes away, as was the fire department. I understood the locks on the doors and windows and how the hidden cameras worked. My neighbor Jax and I had secret code words we changed intermittently so that if we heard them, we'd know to call 911 immediately.

Greg would be out of prison sometime soon. I needed to feel safe.

I loved that Trilby had left me this house, but I didn't know why he'd done it.

Regardless of what his plans had been or, for that matter, what my future ones were, I was here for the night and I was tired. I fed Chloe, then took a shower in the admittedly luxurious bathroom between the bedroom and the office and put on pajama pants and a long-sleeved T-shirt that declared my loyalty to Michigan State—where I'd never gone.

I ate my dinner, then went into the office. There was no harm in familiarizing myself with the computer, was there? It looked like the all-in-one unit I'd been using for a few years. I'd told Trilby if he got any ideas about replacing it, I would quit without notice; it was my favorite of all the ones I'd ever had.

Within minutes, I went to get the flash drives out of the Important Things pocket inside my purse. I came back to the office with the drives, a cup of coffee, and Chloe at my heels. She found a spot on a cushion I laid on the floor and I found one in the desk chair. I slid a drive into the USB port on the back of the big screen in front of me and opened the file I hadn't touched since the day before Trilby died.

Finish what we've started, then go out on your own. Remember to watch the sun. – TW

Trilby had added the words at the stopping point of the manuscript of *Mayhem at the Fair.* He'd urged me in every possible way to be independent, to push myself away from the insulated little life I had in Muskegon. He'd also tried in every possible way to engineer exactly how I should do that very thing.

"Damn you, Trilby," I muttered into the silence, and began to type.

Chapter 3

Sam called in the morning as I was eating my breakfast at the computer and staring out at the six-inch accumulation of snow that had fallen overnight. I'd worked until very late, thrilled with the story and yet dreading its finish because the next one, *Mayhem on Monday*, would be Trilby's last. I was so sleepy when I went to bed that I could barely remember climbing between the soft sheets. When Chloe whimpered from the floor beside the bed, I'd leaned over to pick her up, nearly toppling off the mattress in the process.

I, who never slept well anywhere except in my own bed, slept like the proverbial dead. For ten hours. I could only remember doing that one other time in my life, and I didn't want to think about that.

"Did you know about all this?" I asked Sam. "This house, I mean. This lake."

"That it was going to you? Not until he added it to his will a while back. What do you think of it? The house and the lake, I mean?"

"Well, they're beautiful, of course. But I can't keep them."

"He left that up to you. It wasn't one of those *you have to live in it for a year* things like he put in his Mayhem books. He didn't even leave half of it to me so we could fight over it. I thought that was a little shortsighted of him, but what do I know?"

"What do you think I should do?" I valued his opinion and I trusted him as much I'd trusted anyone in a long time. I didn't think he'd steer me wrong.

"I don't think anything at all," he said promptly.

Not the answer I was looking for.

An unaccustomed sound—what was I saying? Everything here was unaccustomed—came from outside. My heartbeat quickened. "Someone's outside."

Would an unfamiliar sound always bring Greg to mind? Probably. He was out of my life now, but I had no doubt he'd be back. I'm not necessarily that intuitive, but to quote the office manager in Trilby Winterroad's Mayhem books, *I know what I know.*

"Just keep talking and go look outside."

I should have thought of that on my own. Irritated because I hadn't, I went to look out the windows on the driveway side of the house. The sun had come out, weak though it was, and I squinted against it as it bounced off ice-covered tree branches in diamond sparkles, shielding my eyes with a hand on my forehead.

"It's a truck. A big pickup thing." I didn't know one truck from another, although Sam's was black and Trilby's recurring sleuth, Finlay Iverson, drove one whose statistics I could reel off without even looking. I could tell the one in the driveway wasn't like that. For one thing, this one had a V-shaped plow on the front of it and it was clearing the driveway in one trip. I hoped my beloved blue car hadn't hidden itself in the fresh snowfall from the night before.

The truck didn't go back down the sloping drive, and I went to the kitchen to see where it went.

"Someone's plowing the drive," I explained to Sam, peering out the windows like I was Alice Kravitz from the old *Bewitched* show. "He buried my car, and now he's sweeping the snow off and shoveling it out of the way. I parked outside because I didn't know how to get into the garage."

My words fell into silence. For a second, I thought the call had dropped, since I was talking from somewhere in the middle parts of the back of the beyond. But then Sam said, "The lock code on the garage's access door is the same as on the back door to the house. The remote for the overhead doors is in the mudroom on the shelf above the coat hooks; you'll want to put it in your car. There's another one in the garage beside the door closest to the house."

"Oh, okay. Thank you." I'd never had a garage. My apartment building had carports and we each got a space. When it snowed or was icy or both, the products of winter rage magically disappeared.

Then it hit me.

“How do you know that, Sam?” Before he could answer, I said, “Wait a minute. Can you hang on?” I rushed out through the mudroom, realizing as I did so that my soft-soled slippers did little to protect my feet from the snow.

“Thank you,” I said to the man, stopping one of those hair’s breadths from the edge of the step. “How can I pay you?”

“No pay necessary. It’s part of the lake service.” He smiled at me, his cheeks ruddy in the cold. “I’m Jake Crossley. My wife Emily and I do the plowing.”

I told him my name and thanked him again. I wondered if I should offer him something to drink, but didn’t want to invite a stranger inside. However, Sam was on the phone, so surely it would be safe. “Would you like some coffee?”

The smile widened, and I couldn’t help responding to it. “Next time,” he said. “I have a thermos and that will last me until I get to the store to refill it. Thanks, though.” He started toward his truck, then came back. “Mrs. Newland kept a garage door remote in the mudroom. She also had a list of numbers inside the cupboard door of services you might need.”

I thanked him again. Back in the house, oddly pleased with the exchange but finding it strange that everyone seemed to know everything I didn’t, I said to Sam, “You were saying?”

“I wasn’t saying anything.”

"Then it's time you were. How did you know that? Mr. Crossley just told me the very same thing you did."

"Did Jake tell you about the list of numbers, too?"

"Yes." I waited.

"Annabelle Newland was…someone I knew."

I knew, because I knew Sam Eldridge, that I wouldn't learn more. At least not now. "All right," I said. "I know you're not going to tell me any secrets. I do need to know if there are any bodies in the basement or anything like that. Typing Trilby's books all these years has left me with unusual fears." That wasn't true; I was almost fearless. Although Sam knew about the *almost* part.

"No bodies that I know of. I just called to see if you needed anything."

I shook my head, realized he couldn't see me, and said, "No, I'm good."

And I was. It felt good to work, so I put in the same kind of workday I had when Trilby was alive, albeit I started it a couple of hours late and ended it early when Chloe sat at my knee and begged me with chocolate eyes for attention.

"Do you want to walk again?" I asked. I'm a sedentary person by nature—the walk yesterday would have been enough to last me for a week. But then, I'm not a dog.

The sun had melted the ice from the trees and the snow was soft under the soles of my boots. We stayed on the road to walk, as Chloe's short legs sank into the snow when we left it, causing such a look of dismay to cross her face that I burst out laughing.

We walked straight to the store to return the cooler that had held my groceries. The same person was at the counter as had been there the day before, and she offered Chloe a treat before saying, "I made vegetable soup today if you'd like some for your supper."

"That sounds wonderful." And it did. I never cooked much for myself—it wasn't fun to cook for one.

"I'm Rose Harmon. We own the store." She gestured at the golden retriever beside what I think was a woodstove who was making Chloe welcome. "Actually, he does. That's Jim. He just lets my husband and me work here."

Rose was older than me, I think, and looked like someone who worked hard. I know, how can you tell by looking at someone that she works hard? I can't explain it, but I know it. Maybe it was no more than short, unpolished nails and knuckles that bespoke encroaching arthritis on her hands. She was pretty, too, with smiling brown eyes like I'd always wanted. Mine are plain light blue with no exciting flecks or circles of something else. Just like my hair is plain light brown, regardless of how Tim's loving eyes saw it. Neither thick nor thin, curly nor straight. If I were a dog, I'd be a mutt.

I laughed. "Hello, Rose, and hello, Jim. I'm Maggie North and this is Chloe." I was used to friendliness. Muskegon is a welcoming kind of place, but I sensed a difference here. More intimate … or maybe the feeling of listening … attention. I wasn't sure I was comfortable with it.

Rose filled a thermal container with the delicious-smelling soup, then wouldn't let me pay for it. "It's a welcome gift," she said, setting it into a foil-lined shopping bag and handing it to me. "Enjoy it."

"Thank you."

I wasn't used to thanking people so much or, worse, to being beholden to anyone. Like the intimacy of the tiny lake community, it made me uneasy.

Chloe was in no hurry to go back outside, but we left anyway, continuing the trek around the snow-covered lake. I noticed things I'd missed the day before. I hadn't even paid much attention to the second, sparser row of houses and mobile homes that were accessed from the same little road by alley-like streets that looked like driveways.

At the end of the lake, where it trickled off into a creek, a small white church stood in the trees at the top of the hill that rose above the water. A cemetery was visible behind it and a pretty brick house beside it—I wondered if it was the parsonage.

I hadn't attended church since Tim died, but I'd had an unending curiosity about houses of worship since childhood. I also had faith, even if my relationship with it was cantankerous at best.

"Let's go look," I suggested to Chloe, who didn't appear at all excited by the prospect, but followed me up the hill nonetheless.

The church building was small and old and as pristine as it had appeared from the road. Its steps had already been cleaned and its sign invited all comers to attend Sunday morning worship services at nine-thirty each week and coffee at the parsonage on Wednesday afternoon at two P.M. The sign also introduced its pastor as Rev. Carissa D. Newland.

I didn't think I'd ever known anyone with the surname *Newland* before Trilby adopted it for his children's books series, and suddenly it seemed to be everywhere. Well, not everywhere, but certainly around Harper Loch. I remembered the quote from *Alice in Wonderland* about things getting "curiouser and curiouser," and thought I might know how Alice felt.

"May I help you?"

The voice, musical and strong, came from behind me, scaring me so much I nearly fell off the church step. Chloe, however, was delighted. She ran to meet the young woman who approached. She bent to pet the excited dog and caress her ears. "Hi, Chloe. How you doing?" She straightened to greet me. "I'm Carissa Newland. Cari. Would you like to go in?"

I started to demur, but the truth was that I loved churches' interiors as much as their outsides. They all seemed to have a beauty of their own that had little to do with the humans who built them and worshiped within them.

"Yes," I said instead. "Thank you." I extended my hand. "I'm Maggie North."

"Oh, I know. You've been here twenty-four hours. I like to think we don't gossip here on the lake, but we do keep our eyes and ears open." Cari stepped past me to unlock the door. "When I was a kid, coming here to visit my grandparents—those would be the Newlands who lived in your house—the door was always unlocked. Like everywhere else, we can't do that anymore." She moved back to let me go in first, and I stopped almost in her way, my grumpy faith finding me in this little sanctuary that glowed in the light that came through its stained-glass windows. Christ with the lamb was represented in the glass of one of the windows, and His robes were blue. Less dense and warmer than most of the blues in the Burl's windows.

The two rows of old-fashioned pews were of a worn, satiny finish in a wood I was unable to identify, but reminded me of the unpainted cupboards in the Burl. The seats were simple in structure, but beautiful. Hymnals and pew Bibles were in racks on the backs of all but the rows farthest back in the room. The chancel area was plain, with a cross on the wall behind the altar and winter wreaths hanging on the walls at either side. There was no pulpit.

A parlor grand piano filled a corner. It made my fingers itch.

"The pews and the altar are hickory," said Reverend Newland. "From trees out behind your house. Apparently, a whole bunch of them came down in a tornado early in the twentieth century, and the men in the church made good use of the wood. That's why there are imperfections, just like the ones in us. We share faith, but have differences. I know pride is unbecoming, but we're all enormously proud of our pews and our congregation."

"You should be," I said, taking off my glove so I could feel the smooth wood against my hand. "It's beautiful in here. How many does it seat?"

"We can get a hundred in here—it's been done—but it's probably a fire hazard if we do. Attendance runs between twenty and forty. More on Christmas and Easter or when we're combining services with the church in Placer. Fewer if the fish are biting. Oh, and sometimes more when the summer people are here, too."

"No pulpit?"

"I can't stand still."

That didn't surprise me—energy fairly emanated from her. But I couldn't help wondering why I lived in her grandmother's house and she didn't. Working for Trilby had gotten me past the reticence ingrained in me by my upbringing. A writer's most important trait, he always said, was curiosity.

"I feel as if I'm keeping your house from you," I said. "It's such a beautiful place, full of memories and warmth. It should be with family."

"Family didn't want it or couldn't afford it. They were a combined household, and my grandmother—actually my step-grandmother—and grandfather bought the house together when they married. The lake was always her home of choice, but she didn't live in it full-time until Grandpa died. With the family's approval, not to mention their relief, she sold it to Mr. Winterroad."

Little pieces of the mystery that was the Burl fell into place.

"I hope you'll stop by while I'm here," I said. "Maybe you could tell me things about the house. I haven't even explored it all yet."

"I'd like that."

"Thursday for lunch?"

I'd intended to head back to Muskegon on Wednesday morning—tomorrow—but what was one more day? While it was true I was a creature of routine, it was also true that I no longer had one. I also wanted to cook something in that kitchen before I left.

"Sounds great."

I complained to Chloe all the way back to the Burl. "I'm not even sociable with people I *know*," I said, being careful not to gesture with the container of soup. I didn't want to lose any of it. "So what am I doing inviting a preacher I don't even know to lunch?" I hesitated, almost stumbling. "She knew you, didn't she, Chloe?"

The dachshund bounced off ahead of me toward the house, and the realization that I'd probably bored her made me laugh even as curiosity grew.

I took the soup with me into the office. I was still catching up on the emails that had stuffed both my personal and business accounts since Trilby's death. Chloe settled into the cushion I'd been moving from room to room and closed her eyes. I hadn't thought to bring her bed from Muskegon for only a few days.

Sales of Trilby's backlist had increased almost on a daily basis since he died. The publisher and agent were discussing rereleases of his earlier works. I had the title, notes, and outline of one more book after *Mayhem at the Fair* was completed. I could write it—of course I could. I'd been Finlay Iverson's voice for a while now. I'd come up with *great Santa's beard*, the oath he adopted to cut back on swearing. The stories came to Trilby just as they always had, but during the last ten years, since Claire's initial diagnosis, he'd been unable to write them.

I had always been Paris Newland, from the very day Trilby sat on the corner of my desk and said, "What would you think of a children's series?"

He'd presented it to his agent and publisher and they had been thrilled, but not with the idea of my name being on the cover, so the Lunchroom Mysteries were released with PARIS NEWLAND as the author. That Paris Newland was actually Trilby Winterroad became one of the worst-kept secrets in all of publishing.

It was the best of situations for me. I loved the work, but had no wish for readers to know who I was. Trilby kept his private and public lives separate, but it was often difficult. As his assistant and ghost writer, I neither had nor wanted a public life, and my personal one was … well, mine.

I remembered the binder that held all the notes on *Mayhem on Monday* and wondered what I should do when it was done.

What would become of Finlay Iverson? And what would become of me?

Chapter 4

I decided to go to coffee at the parsonage on Wednesday afternoon. I'd had absolutely no intention of going, but I was annoyed because the internet decided to take a break from Harper Loch when I needed it to go on with what I was doing—which was checking my frequent confusion of the use of *who* and *whom*. The young rural mail carrier, who drove a Jeep with a steering wheel on the wrong side and introduced himself as Flynn Squires, came to the back door because I didn't hear him honk his horn. Who knew they didn't just dump things on the porch and leave? He delivered an Express Mail envelope to me in exchange for my signature and said his wife informed him he was supposed to invite me to coffee at the parsonage whether I had any mail or not.

"I've only been here three nights, and hardly anyone knows I'm here," I said, laughing, as I signed for the Tyvek envelope. "I'm surprised to even get this. Thank your wife, though. What's her name?"

He grinned back at me, the expression reminding me of the young man who delivered my groceries. "Amy Squires. You'll know her because she's the only pregnant woman on the lake."

"Is Eamon your brother?"

"He is. A good kid, that one, although I still tell Mom she should have stopped with me when she knew she'd achieved perfection. Oh." He rummaged in his pocket. "Here's the Scripture for today. The gathering isn't a Bible study, but Cari likes to get her professional licks in anyway."

The only Bible I had was Tim's, and it was at home in the cedar chest that had been my mother's. I worried about that for a few minutes. I had kept it, hadn't I? Our wedding date was recorded in it, and the day of Tim's death. Not that I was likely to forget either event, but I needed to hold the memories of our life together close. They were the good days, the days that shone blue in my heart.

In the meantime, I had to open the envelope from the agent. I always refer to Mikayla Fenton as "the agent" or "Trilby's agent," but the truth is she's mine, too, and has been through all the Paris Newland books.

The envelope held official paperwork and Miki's offer to continue to represent me through the publication of the final Mayhem books. At the end of the included note, she added,

When you decide to write as yourself, regardless of the name you choose to use, get with me on what you want to do. We've been selling your voice for a long time—I think that can continue.

Could it? Trilby had suggested more than once that I seek publication on my own. A part of me had wanted to, but another part—the pragmatic part—understood that I made much better money under the umbrella carried by Trilby Winterroad and Paris Newland than I would writing the historical romance novels that owned my reader's heart. Besides, I liked my life being private without my having to work at maintaining it.

I was having some trouble thinking about work. About my future. I liked Harper Loch. I'd say it felt like home, but that would be ridiculous; I've lived in Muskegon my whole life. It *is* home.

But *home* has more than one definition, doesn't it? It's the place you live, where your clothes are in the closet and the silverware is in a certain drawer and your mail gets delivered every day. Your bed is there and framed photographs and the thermostat that keeps you comfortable. When you head back to it after having been away, you say you're going home and there's reassurance in that word. You're going to be warm and safe and know where thc spoons are.

Sometimes, though, it's the place that holds your heart. The little three-bedroom ranch house Tim and I were saving for all those years ago is still home in that pocket of my heart that will forever belong to him. For years, I wouldn't drive past it. I can now, and I can do it without crying. But I still think of being there with him, standing outside and talking about how we'd paint the shutters and have flower boxes on all the windows. I still think of how the five years of our marriage meant more to me than the forty-seven other years of my life.

He wouldn't like that. He'd say, *Good grief, Margaret Mary, get over yourself!*

The duplex where I'd grown up wasn't there anymore, and neither were the people who raised me. They hadn't wanted kids, but then Aunt Lin's brother and sister-in-law had been killed in a car wreck and there I was: a solemn five-year-old with nowhere to go. I remembered my real parents a little, but it was Aunt Lin and Uncle Bill who did the legwork. They loved me in spite of themselves, and I loved them back, but they were glad when I was grown up and so was I. They retired to Arizona five years ago. We talk often and I fly out to see them at least once every year. We love each other, but the connection is distant. If it's possible to be connected *and* distant, I mean.

That love we share doesn't make the place I grew up *home,* especially since its address is part of an apartment complex now. The condo I bought as an investment hadn't been home either. Everything was white or beige, glass and stainless steel. I knew when Tom and Dan brought their kids there and I worried about them spilling stuff that it was never going to be a place of warmth and welcome. After Greg, even the investment no longer mattered.

But now there's the house on the lake. I haven't even been in the attic or the basement yet, and the Burl is vastly bigger than anything I'll ever need, but there's something about its lack of symmetry and kaleidoscope of colors. About the blue I see in every room.

So here I was, walking through the melting snow to the parsonage, which was indeed the redbrick house beside the church. Rose Harmon was just ahead of me on the shoveled path. A young woman who must be Amy Squires was behind me. Everyone waved cheerfully, but concentrated on where they were going.

The house was cozy and although it wasn't very big, it was arranged for gathering and counseling. Cari's office off the living room had a comfortable seating area and a prayer kneeler beneath a leaded glass window that reminded me of the ones at the Burl. A convenient powder room opened onto the hallway. The kitchen was no more than a galley, but the dining room easily accommodated a long table made from what Rose said was yet another fallen hickory tree.

There were eight of us. We all had steaming cups of tea, coffee, or mulled cider, and there was a platter of cookies in the middle of the table so full that its weight should have cracked the wood.

They talked like girlfriends do. When the conversation turned to love, it was palpable in the conversation. Amy's long-wanted pregnancy. Rose and Colby's rescue of a marriage gone south. Cari's reluctant acquiescence to the call of the pastorate. Emily Crossley's transition from a CEO in Grand

Rapids to a snowplow and lawn tractor operator on Harper Loch.

The last one threw me. “Really?” I said, breaking my silence. “Willingly?”

“Oh, goodness, no, but when my company took its operations overseas and I didn’t want to go with it, I was left with a hefty severance and no plans. Jake took a semester off teaching school and we came down here to fix up Cross My Heart cottage while I made up my mind what to do. When it snowed the first time, Jake informed me it was fine to feel sorry for myself, but it wasn’t going to be on his time. The homeowners’ association already had the equipment, so we took over the snowplowing. When spring came and we still hadn’t made up our minds, we took up the mowing, too. He got a teaching job at Placer and I do some consulting from home. Now I don’t remember why I didn’t want to leave the city.”

Strangely enough, I could understand that. It wasn’t going to happen to me, but I certainly did have a voice running around in my head saying *Why the hell not?* regardless of where I was either physically or mentally. Looking around at these women, including the pastor at the head of the table, I doubted my unspoken curse word would have surprised any of them. My life wasn’t the only one that had not moved in a straight line.

"I was in culinary school in Chicago," said Cari, "and I was sure either God was mistaken or I was hearing wrong. I thought I could become a chef in a Christian restaurant. Surely that would be enough." She shrugged. "It wasn't."

"We do stand in line to get a helping of whatever she cooks for church dinners," said Rose, and everyone laughed.

Seriously? And I'd invited her to lunch?

They were all friendly. They reminded me of the four of us from high school who occasionally gather back in Muskegon. We are all single, have pasts we don't always like to visit, and have made what we consider to be decent lives on our own. In truth, I think I'm the only one who actually *likes* being single, but the other three have chosen it rather than risk history repeating itself.

Most of these women were married, other than Cari and Haley Squires, who was Eamon and Flynn's mother. I would never get everyone's name straight, that much was obvious, much less the names of ones who weren't there. Haley was very quiet and I wondered if the boys had gotten their ebullience from their father. I didn't know whether she was widowed or divorced, and I wondered if she was at a crossroads much as I was.

The gathering ended an hour and fifteen minutes after it started. When we walked back to our houses, we walked together in twos, depending on where we lived. Haley fell into step beside me, and I remembered that she lived in the pretty yellow house two doors away from the Burl. “The Bee,” I said aloud.

“Yes. The boys named it. Flynn wanted to put black stripes on it, but we caught him in time.”

I laughed. Trilby had put some of his own sons’ pranks into books and the additions had been so popular Tom and Dan had asked for a share of royalties in addition to thanks on the acknowledgments page.

Chloe was sleeping in the kitchen rocker when I got back to the house, but she woke as soon as I opened the door to the mudroom and ran right over my feet to get outside. When she came back in, I gave her a snack and made myself some coffee to take into the office with me. It had been a nice afternoon.

“Okay, so you’ve decided to stay the weekend. You going to invite me to see the house?”

I was setting the table in the sunny nook in the kitchen for my lunch with Cari. I put Ellie on speaker phone while I got the pot roast out of the oven. Pretty substantial for a lunch, but I was never willing to fix one for myself and the leftovers would last me several days. “Yes, by all mean, I’d love to have you see it.”

Ellie knew me better than almost anyone. Maybe she'd be able to offer some insight about what I should do with the Burl. Every hour I spent in it made me more reluctant to leave it, but...honestly, what would a fifty-two-year-old single woman want with a big house in the country? I wondered for the hundredth time in the past three days what Trilby had been thinking.

Sun on the colors in the transoms over the kitchen windows made me stop and revel in the dappled warmth of it. *Sun? What did you mean, Trilby?*

"I'll come over after work tomorrow then and stay till Sunday afternoon if that's okay with you."

"Sure is," I said cheerfully, surprised by how okay it was. I wanted to show her my lake. *The* lake, I mean. Not mine. I don't *have* a lake. I have a two-bedroom apartment with a balcony big enough for two chairs and a tiny table between them where I can see a *real* lake if I lean just right.

"Okay. Is it on GPS or will I be out there in the wind and the wilderness and end up buried in a snowdrift where no one will find me until April?"

Her Friday workday ended at noon. I calculated the time it had taken me to get to the lake. "Gladys got me here, so it's on GPS, although you have to argue with it a little bit or you might end up in the water. If you're not here by five, I'll call out the rescue squad." Not that

I was sure they had one, unless Jake and Emily came with the snowplow.

"Hmm…is there pizza delivery? I'll be ready for it."

I thought Eamon Squires might drive to Placer and pick it up for me, but I wasn't asking. "Afraid not, but I have some good wine and the makings for pizza from scratch." At least, I would after another walk to the store. Maybe the mercantile had pizza—they certainly had almost everything else I wanted.

"Healthy?"

"Absolutely not."

"I'm in."

I was learning rather quickly that despite the fact that the Burl and nearly all the other houses on the first row of the lake faced the road, and a lot of residents used their back doors. It made sense when the visitor was driving, because the parking area was in the back of most of the houses, but I didn't understand why anyone would go all the way around back if they were on foot. When Cari's knock came at the back door, I asked her the question.

"Because," she said, "at the lake coat hooks, shoe mats, and mudrooms are always in the back. You're not as likely to have muddy or snowy feet in areas that have sidewalks, whereas most of us don't have sidewalks at all, except for the bigger houses, like the Burl and Lark Meadow."

"Oh." I hadn't thought of that. I have known, and snickered at, occupants of Trilby's circle of friends who have no idea how people lived outside their own rarified circumstances. I wouldn't have thought being an inveterate apartment-dweller would place me in that classification, but maybe it did.

I frowned. "Lark Meadow?"

"The big white house straight across the lake from you."

I'd noticed it even though it was even more deeply in the trees than the Burl or the church were. It reminded me of an antebellum Southern mansion someone had set down and not known where they left it.

"It's like living in a park," I said, apropos of nothing. "Except most parks don't have churches or stores that deliver or eighty-six people who live in them."

"Eighty-five." Cari raised an eyebrow in thanks as she accepted the glass of wine I handed her.

"I read that it was eighty-six."

"My grandmother died last fall and the woman who owns her house hasn't committed to staying here."

"Give me a break," I protested. "I've only been here three days. And I'm staying the weekend, too. My friend Ellie's coming for a few days' R and R and to tell me what I should do—not that I will ask her, but she'll tell me anyway."

Cari beamed. "We all need a friend like that. At least one."

As we ate our roast and the crusty bread I'd made from a loaf of frozen dough I'd gotten at the mercantile, I learned that Cari had come to the lake from Vermont a few years before to spend time with her grandmother, Mrs. Newland. She'd arrived with a broken heart, three swimsuits, and an as-yet-unused clerical collar. When the pastorate at the church opened up, the parishioners invited her to fill the void.

I couldn't explain my interest in the eighty-six people who lived here full-time. Pardon me, eighty-five. Not only my interest, but Chloe's as well. She'd spent all her time with Trilby and me; when others had visited the condo in Muskegon, she'd gone to the closet in the office and stayed there until they left. However, when we walked here, she with her sporty little booties and sweater, she greeted everyone as if they were her long-lost best friends.

Since the Burl had been Cari's grandparents' house, we toured it after lunch. There were five bedrooms upstairs and three bathrooms. None of the bedrooms were very large, but their windows gave them a sense of openness. "This was the sewing room until they built the quilt room at the end of this hall," Kari said in the smallest of the rooms. "My grandfather could never understand why Grannabelle liked to sew when she could buy whatever she wanted, but he made sure she had a good place to do it."

The attic was finished, tall enough to stand up in, and empty except for a few trunks pushed up against one of the knee walls.

"I don't know," said Cari in response to my questioning look. "I haven't been up here since I was a kid, and it was full of stuff then. I know Grannabelle spent a lot of time doing a big cleanout after Grandpa died years ago. Whenever any grandkids were around, she had us carry stuff either up or down to the ground floor."

I wondered who Annabelle Newland's other relatives were, but no one seemed to be saying and I liked my own privacy enough that I wasn't going to go digging around in anyone else's. I have to admit, though, that my interest in Harper Loch and its inhabitants is growing beyond all reason. Trilby had always been appalled by my lack of curiosity. Wouldn't he be surprised if he could see me now?

Besides the plumbing and cooling system, a water conditioner, and two water heaters, the partial basement of the Burl had a wine cellar in one corner. It was all very clean, but there was nothing of real interest beyond the walkout exit that opened onto a cement patio.

“It’s such a warm place,” said Cari, when we’d gone back up to the kitchen, “even with the personal things gone from it. Are you sure you don’t want to stay here, Maggie?”

That was the thing, I realized, pouring the last of the wine into our glasses and handing Cari hers. I wasn’t really sure at all.

Chapter 5

I was glad to see Ellie Friday night. She stopped at Josetta's and bought herself a quilt just as I had. While she was at it, she bought me another one. "It's the flower garden pattern, the lady told me," she said, "and it had all those colors in it. So, happy birthday."

I loved the coverlet. I carried it with me when I showed her upstairs. "This will look wonderful in your room, but does this mean I have to give back the shoes you gave me on my real birthday?" I'm notoriously cheap when it comes to buying shoes, and Ellie knows it. She buys me ones I covet but won't purchase for myself.

"No. The quilt is for this year." Ellie went to the other side of the queen size sleigh bed. "Let's see if it fits."

"It will." I took off the generic white comforter. "We'll leave this in the chest in case you need it." All the bedrooms had chests at the ends of the beds, another thing that charmed me about this house I didn't want.

The one at the end of my bed in the Burl was what's known as a dower chest, although Aunt Lin had always referred to hers as a hope chest. This one reminded me of Pennsylvania Dutch artisanship I'd seen on a research trip for *Mayhem in Bucks County*.

The chest had a glorious sunburst on its top, while a row of flowers was painted around its sides.

"Oh, it's wonderful." Ellie stood back to look at the bed we'd just remade in her room, then stepped into the bathroom. "You even hung new towels and left me a little basket of fun things. When did you become such a good hostess?"

"When you bought me a quilt," I said reasonably and inaccurately. "Does everything look okay? I'm new at this."

"I love it, and I love this house." She grinned wickedly. "Do they really call that a lake here? I can see right across it and almost from one end to the other. And why is it called *loch* instead of *lake*? That seems pretentious."

"Not to the Scots family named Harper who discovered it," I maintained. "I heard all about it at the parsonage on Wednesday. I think the Harpers spent the rest of their lives insisting to non-Scottish people that it was l-o-c-h, not l-o-c-k. Never mind them having to explain why they didn't just say lake."

"Did you say the parsonage?" Ellie raised her eyebrows. She knew I hadn't been to church in a long, long time, other than to see her kids get baptized or to attend a wedding or funeral.

"Cari, the pastor, reminds me of you," I said. "She's pushy."

"So, are you going to church Sunday, since you're here?" asked Ellie, hanging a few clothes in the roomy closet.

"No, you're here." Which was good. I had nothing to wear … at least, not really. And I wasn't interested in going to church at this point, although I really liked the piano.

"As usual, I traveled with black dress pants and a very nice sweater, so I'm good to go."

I sighed. Me, too, and Ellie knew it. We'd both learned it from the same home economics teacher in high school. In truth, that particular uniform stayed packed in my burnt orange overnighter, including a pair of black flats that were so pliable they took up hardly any room when I folded them into the side pocket.

"So, what's for dinner?" she asked. "Are we cooking? Is it pizza?"

"We are and it's not. Not this meal, anyway." The kitchen was so much fun to work in, plus this was my second opportunity in two days to cook for more than one person. My aunt liked to cook, but Uncle Bill *loved* it. I'd learned how from him. We used to make Aunt Lin laugh when we cooked together.

I hadn't thought of that in a long time. Cooking for one held little appeal, but it only took one other person to make it a party. I had indeed bought the ingredients for pizza, but the pasta selection at the mercantile had drawn my attention while I was there.

"You can just sit and watch," I said. "You worked today. I haven't. Or you can take Chloe out. She knows where to go."

"I'll do that." She went into the mudroom and pulled on her coat. "Come on, Chloe. Show me your facilities."

While they were out, Aunt Lin called. I set out a plate of crudités while I was on speaker phone. She talked about pickleball and her quilt club and we laughed about Uncle Bill's golf antics. I told her about the house, planning which room I would make into theirs if I could get them to visit.

I didn't even remind myself I had no reason to keep the house. The repetition in my mind was driving me crazy.

We finished our call as Ellie and Chloe came in. I said, "Ellie says hello. Love you both, Aunt Lin."

For just a second or so, there was silence, then she said, "Hello back to her. Love you, too, sweetheart."

We so seldom said that to each other. We were not demonstrative as a family. I hadn't always been kissed goodnight or tucked in as a child, although ... I had to think about it a minute to remember, but then I did. I'd had trouble reading at first, so we read together at night around the fireplace—even when there wasn't a fire.

We would take turns. How tired they must have gotten of reading the *Dick and Jane* series Aunt Lin had found at a yard sale, and how relieved she was when every volume of the *Raggedy Ann* books showed up at a used bookstore. I still had those books. Not *Dick and Jane*—we'd worn them out—but the series about the rag doll and Andy, her cohort, who had candy hearts inside the stuffing of their chests.

I had a terrible urge to cry, and I wasn't even sure why.

"How's the book coming?" asked Ellie, making herself a cup of coffee from the single-cup coffeemaker on the coffee bar. "And what are you going to do when it's done?"

I should have known she'd be the one to push that particular button. She was one of the few people who knew for sure I'd been Trilby's ghostwriter. He hadn't cared much, but I'd wanted to protect his literary reputation. He'd given so much to the genres he wrote in that I couldn't bear to have that gift lessened.

"I don't know."

I didn't have to do anything. Money wasn't an issue and I was sure the value of this house would create a nest egg on its own if I decided to sell it.

I had to admit that was looking less likely with every passing hour.

"Not that I haven't mentioned this before, but why don't you give writing as Maggie Wallace a shot, like you used to talk about when we were in high school? Or Maggie North, for that matter? I know you've never done that—at least, that I know of—but I have no doubt you could. There's a lot of you in the Mayhem books, and the Lunchroom Mysteries were all you."

Ellie was an avid reader. She'd read Trilby's books, too, including both series. She was always amazed that she couldn't tell which ones I'd written and which ones he had, but that had been the idea, after all. Although I read a lot, too, I leaned toward women's fiction and romance. When I was writing for Trilby, I had to stay away from reading mysteries; I couldn't stay with Trilby's voice if someone else's was in my head at the same time.

"I brought a sack of books I've read recently with me. Why don't you give them a look? Especially the cozies."

I slid the manicotti I'd decided on into the oven and joined her at the table, making myself a cup of tea at the coffee bar. Earl Grey and I were close friends in the evening. "I've been sitting in front of a computer since I was sixteen. Maybe it's time to do something else." I didn't think so, but it was a thought.

"Hmm … okay." She subsided, which didn't mean a thing. Ellie had raised two kids, largely on her own—

she knew how to get to the heart of matters others might prefer to leave alone.

"So," she said, "have you met anyone single since we've seen each other?"

I sighed. "No, and I haven't tried."

"Don't let Greg Mathis set the limits for the rest of your life, Maggie."

He already had, and I'd let it happen. We'd been divorced for seven years after having only being married for two, but those twenty-some months laid some ugly groundwork I didn't have the courage to escape.

"It's such a joke, isn't it? One of those things that happens to people you don't know," I said. I'd typed those very words not two days before it happened. *You can't rape your own wife.* "He'll be out of jail soon, Ellie, if he's not already. What am I going to do?"

There. I'd said it. I'd vocalized the only thing in the world I'm afraid of for myself. I worry about my aunt and uncle, about Ellie and her family, and Trilby's family, and Sam. But in my mind the worst had already happened to me was when I lost Tim.

Except for Greg.

Ellie was silent. I wasn't the only abused woman she'd taken care of as a nurse practitioner or whose behalf she'd represented in court when asked, but it had been harder because we were friends. She'd done more than her part—I shouldn't lean on her now.

I shouldn't lean on anyone. I knew that. "I'll be fine," I said. "It's good to be aware, and I am, but I'll be fine."

If I said it often enough, it would be true, right?

"It's a reason not to go back to Muskegon," Ellie said slowly. "He'll find you too easily there. I know you live in a building with security measures in place, but will you end up afraid to leave your apartment in case he's lying in wait? The wrong person would be in prison then, wouldn't she?"

"It's not prison, living in a small circle. I like not going out." Small circle. Small life. I've always spent most of my time by myself. I don't like eating alone in restaurants very much, so I usually don't, and I never go to coffee shops or bars unless I'm with Ellie and sometimes the friends from school we socialize with. I loved spending time with Trilby and Claire at their country house, but I was always relieved to be back in my quiet apartment.

I'm not agoraphobic, although I suppose I came close to it after the experience with Greg. I lived between Trilby's condo and my new apartment for the most part after he'd been arrested. When the corona virus created a pandemic, I learned the dubious joy of having virtually everything delivered.

"The only real difference will be that I'll look over my shoulder more when I do go out," I said. "I have no reason to think he'll come back to Muskegon."

Ellie didn't have to say the words that lay between us like the vegetable tray on the table. I didn't have to think he'd come back to Muskegon. I knew he would.

On Saturday, Ellie and I went to Placer, which is, as Flynn told me when he delivered yet another Express Mail, it's only about a mile and a half as the crow flies. "That means in good weather, you can ride a bike or take a golf cart along Oxley's Ditch Road and get there in the same amount of time, but have more pleasure in the trip. It's a private road past his farm, but everyone uses it."

But I wouldn't be here in good weather. By that time, Greg would certainly be out of prison. I didn't think I'd ever feel safe again, but at least I'd be back in my apartment building with its twenty-four-seven security. Hopefully he'd return to Chicago, where he'd lived when Trilby introduced us. Not that Chicago was far enough away to allow me to feel a semblance of safety, but it was a place I never went.

We left the car in the parking lot by the bank and walked around, since the day was warm enough that dripping sounds were everywhere. "I never knew you could hear snow melt," I said.

Ellie gave me an admiring look. "That's very poetic-sounding."

I smacked her arm and she pushed me so that I ended up leaning against a lamppost laughing. She took my picture with her phone, then started walking again. I had to run to catch up.

She took notes as we went. Placer had a clinic on the edge of town, staffed by both a physician and a nurse practitioner. A dentist's office and a vision center were in a downtown building, each of them open two days a week. A small supermarket promised fresh meat, locally grown and butchered, and a well-stocked deli. Webb Pharmacy was on one corner, IN BUSINESS SINCE 1896. Josetta's quilt shop and a branch library anchored two more corners. I was relieved to see a gas station-convenience store combination. A chain dollar store was across the street from a veterinary clinic.

We saw three churches, which I thought was a lot for a town with a thousand people in it. One of them was the same denomination as the one I wasn't going to the next day out at the lake. Another was Lutheran, and the third was possibly the smallest and prettiest Catholic Church I'd ever seen. St. Robert's made me wish I was Catholic, even though I was divorced and a feminist. The fact that I thought Bing Crosby really was a priest until I went to college probably wouldn't speak well for my devotion, either, and we won't even talk about the abortion thing. While I never took advantage of it, I took for granted my rights over my own body were sacrosanct.

High Street was two long blocks of big old houses, complete with cobblestone sidewalks and a grassy median dividing the street. The homes were much more elegant than the Burl, although no bigger, and they reminded me of the movies from the middle of the twentieth century that Aunt Lin and I used to watch on TV. I'd seen *Cheaper by the Dozen* and *Meet Me in St. Louis* often enough I knew a lot of the dialogue by heart.

The town even had a park.

Oh, how could it be? I *love* parks. However, I'd pretty much stopped going to the beautiful parks in Muskegon after Greg. Even if I was riding my bike, I always felt as if someone was right behind me or spying on me from the tall branches of trees I rode under.

Placer Village Park was small, taking up just a block near the edge of town, but it was so pretty it made my heart twist. A gazebo sat in the middle, with sidewalks going out from it like spokes from a wheel toward a playground, tennis and pickleball courts, a parking lot, and a few pavilions of different sizes. A walking path, much like the road at the lake only narrower, meandered all the way around the park. At the park's edge, making it appear bigger, was a youth baseball park.

By the time we returned to the car, the sun had tumbled into the horizon. Kristy's Hometown Café had all-you-could-eat fried chicken, so we stuffed ourselves before driving back to the Burl.

Ellie went to bed early, blaming overexposure to country air and chicken legs, and I put on sweats and went into the office. The envelope from Sam was there, unopened.

I felt a sudden longing to see him. Our friendship is so one-sided, though. Because he's been my lawyer ever since he passed the Michigan bar, he knows all there is to know about me. He keeps it to himself and never mentions anything unless it's for my good.

I, on the other hand, know very little about him. He's been married once, but I never met his wife. He likes to play golf, watch college football, fish, and cook. He hikes and backpacks with friends, and is often gone for days at a time. He lives in a condo close to Trilby's and has what he calls a vague, lazy interest in politics. He reads incessantly. If he has family, I don't know it. I think his parents were friends with Trilby and Claire, but I'm not sure of that. I never knew them. I don't know where he grew up. He's a partner in his law firm, but he avoids the social part every chance he gets. He says he's learned that from me.

I texted him, suddenly anxious. Whether it was because of the unopened Express Mail or because I didn't know where his home of origin was, I couldn't have said. I GOT THE ENVELOPE BUT HAVEN'T OPENED IT YET. WHERE DID YOU GROW UP?

The answer came in seconds. OPEN IT. IT WON'T BITE. VERMONT.

I opened the envelope, finding copies of my will reflecting the changes I made after Trilby's death. Had he really only been gone a month? I folded a copy into an envelope to send home with Ellie, then put the others in a folder I had ready to take with me when I left the Burl.

At the bottom of the thin stack of papers from the envelope was a recipe for garlic-cheddar biscuits with a note at the bottom. *I've been in the kitchen of the Burl—what a chef's delight! Invite me for dinner and I'll help you cook. Something to go with these.*

The recipe looked good. The idea of inviting him to dinner sounded…

I stopped mid-thought. It sounded too much like I intended to keep this house.

The folder holding the copies of the will and the contract from Miki was one of the flowered ones I favored. It lay in front of me. Thoughtful, silent, I closed it and slipped it into the security drawer in the desk.

I settled in at the computer to write for an hour or two. There was no hurry, really—I had months before the deadline—but a part of me wanted it to be done. I'd never felt like an imposter when I wrote according to Trilby's plan, but I did now. I missed being able to ask him questions, to laugh with him about Finlay Iverson's quirks. On the day this book was finished, I would miss celebrating with him even though there was another book left to write.

It was complicated, my relationship with Trilby. There'd been nothing remotely sexual about it, nor anything paternal—although my age fell between Tom's and Dan's. He was the only boss I ever had and, in some ways, the best friend.

He'd never forgiven himself for introducing me to his brother, adopted by his parents after Trilby was grown.

I had to stop my train of thought right dead in the middle of its tracks, something I'd learned to do post-Greg. If I hadn't, I don't know how I would have survived. Sometimes, when I thought of the near-recluse I had become, I wasn't really sure I *had* survived. Not completely, anyway.

With a few hundred words added to the manuscript, I checked the alarm system—for the first time since I'd come to Harper Loch. Satisfied, I checked the locks and turned off all but what I'd termed the "running lights" in this big house. Chloe fell into step beside me as I went to the bedroom.

I fell asleep quickly, as I had the other nights I'd spent here, glad Ellie was in the house. Glad Chloe was in the room. I would be fine. I'd go back to Muskegon in a few days, back to my secure building where hardly anyone but Jax, the neighbor across the hall, knew my name. Which was okay—I didn't know theirs, either.

Greg would be released soon. Or had he already been? Would they contact me when he was? I thought so, but I wasn't sure. Things fell through the cracks all the time.

All the time.

Chapter 6

Regardless of my several-times-stated intent otherwise, Ellie and I went to church on Sunday morning, sliding into one of the polished pews and waving back at people who waved at us. Although the order of worship was somewhat different than in the church where I grew up, was married in, and buried Tim from, the music was the same. The promotional fans in the pew racks with hymnals and offering envelopes were the same.

No one played the beautiful piano. The music itself was recorded. In all fairness, it was cued perfectly and the sound system was pretty good. But still.

My fingers itched. I'd played the one at the Burl every day since I'd gotten here—each time to the point that I had to take some pain relievers to ease the ache in my hands. I'd played hymns at my aunt and uncle's church. I could probably do it again, although not with the certainty that I could play other things. I thought of "The Entertainer." Tim and I had played that together, laughing and pushing each other off the piano bench.

The congregation interceded for those with concerns and celebrated for those who had praises, up to and including Emily's grandson being on the second-grade honor roll, I prayed for that memory with Tim to stay alive in me forever.

Being in church felt good—there was no denying it. Did I feel like I belonged there? No, I don't think so. A sense of belonging had eluded me most of my life—why would things be any different now?

We had leftover manicotti and pizza for lunch, then Ellie set out for Muskegon. I wrote more on *Mayhem at the Fair*, thinking I might stay here long enough to finish it. It would only take a few days, and then I could start on *Mayhem on Monday*. The last book.

Trilby had died on a Monday. What a terrible joke, and I had no doubt he'd meant it as such. *Lighten up, Maggie.*

As often happened, once I got started, I didn't want to stop. The shadows were deep by the time Chloe reminded me rather desperately that she wanted to go outside. The lights on Enoch Trace were coming on slowly, the soft illumination following the narrow serpentine road around the lake,

There were not enough of the old-fashioned lampposts to make the trek around Harper Loch inviting to strangers, Colby Harmon had explained to me while he wrapped the cheese I bought to make the manicotti. They were there simply to keep lake people from stepping in potholes when they walked.

I was amazed by how many people I'd come to recognize in the few days I'd been at Harper Loch. It is a place of walkers, joggers, bicyclists. Not that they all live at the lake; some of them park at the mercantile and take off from there. Golf carts are frequent, considering the sparsity of the population, and legal. There was one in the Burl's garage.

Not everybody walks along the road. The path at the edge of the lake is well-worn, with an occasional park bench offering respite. From what I've seen, quite a few of the eighty-five full-timers are at least as old as I am. A few young people, like Flynn and Amy, live in houses that had belonged to their grandparents or in mobile homes on the second row. Although there is plenty of room around the lake for new construction, what Cari calls the Law of the Land and Water limits it. The Burl is on a huge lot, and it's not the only one that is.

In a wealthier, more urban area, Harper Loch would be a gold mine for a developer. The thought made me shudder. Not that I don't like cities—I do, as long as I don't have to do much driving in them. And I love everything Muskegon offers. But I'd hate to see this little country lake become anything different from what it is.

As Chloe and I meandered in the direction of the mercantile, I heard footsteps behind me on the asphalt, moving faster than I was. I shortened Chloe's leash and moved to the edge of the road, conscious of my heartbeat accelerating to a point I felt breathless with it.

While I'm not timid, except perhaps where violent ex-husbands are concerned, I'm not unaware, either. My hand clamped around the pepper spray can in my pocket.

Bad things happen.

"On your right," said a voice, sounding more breathless than I felt, and the person jogged past me, slowing enough to give Chloe's head a pat and me a nod. He wore clothes with reflective stripes on them.

My heart was still beating harder and faster, and I turned back toward the house, the pleasure in the walk spoiled by my own paranoia.

"Maggie!"

I turned, relieved by the familiarity of the voice.

"Wait up," said Cari, speeding her steps to reach me. "I meant to ask you this morning if you wanted to join the late-day walkers, but you and your friend got away too fast. We walk most evenings, but not always at the same time. We're early today. We have a text group, and the first one to hit the road sends out the signal. Sometimes we're all there, sometimes just two, but the truth is that in the social and political climate of the country these days, walking alone isn't always that comfortable." She beamed. "Of course, it's safe for me, because pastors have special dispensation, but for you laypeople—"

She was interrupted by derisive hooting from the ones accompanying her, and, surprising myself, from me—I'm not the hooting type. Four of the group were there tonight. Rose was one, Cari another, and I didn't recognize the other two.

One of them, slim and pretty and elegant, extended her hand. "I'm Dallas Comerford. I run the Lavender Park Salon." She elbowed the woman beside her. "This is Sadie Laughlin. She's the librarian in Placer."

I introduced myself, and we walked on. Chloe had fallen in love with Cari when the pastor came for lunch, so she was thrilled to walk with her instead of me. Conversation was minimal, but when Cari started singing "Old Time Rock and Roll," we joined in one-by-one.

Yeah, me, too. I'm no more a public singer than I am a hooter, but there you go. This was the lake. I hadn't walked with four people at the same time since elementary school, and I'd never done it by choice. Alone had always been easier.

I'm not very good at conversation. Aunt Lin has always apologized to me for that, because she isn't either. Even when it was time to discuss things like periods and sex and birth control, she gave me books and told me there were questions and answers at the end of each one. Ellie always said it didn't matter because she talked enough for both of us. She does, but she's a great listener too.

So was Tim. When I explained to him about writing prompts, which Trilby sometimes used just to get Finlay going on the right path, he immediately came up with the idea of conversation prompts to get me to talk. They worked wonders, and we talked all the time.

When we reached the Lavender Park Salon, Dallas invited us in for hot chocolate. Her husband was an over-the-road trucker, gone more than he was home, and had already left for the week. "I don't mind being alone," she said, when we were seated around the oak table in her cozy kitchen while she heated milk. "Trey has been a truckdriver our entire married life. But the first night is always kind of a long one."

I wanted to ask questions about the lake. How did a trucker and a hair stylist afford a house on a lake, even a small one? Why were so many of the cottages painted in crayon-box colors? Not that I objected—I liked the brightness—but they were really…bright. Who lived in the big white house across from the Burl, the one called Lark Meadow? Or did anybody?

Was there a tragedy surrounding the property so that no one ever stayed in the house? That thought sent me down a familiar path. Had there been a murder? A drowning that wasn't an accident?

That kind of curiosity went against my quiet nature, although Trilby had often brought it to life when he talked to me about the Mayhem books while I typed them. Rather than ask people things, though—because that meant talking to them—I'd become a Google devotee from the first time I looked something up.

I felt as if I could ask these women those questions. But I couldn't just jump into the conversation they were having with them, could I? I needed to…

"You wear a wedding ring," said Dallas, gesturing at my hand when she set the tray of mugs of chocolate on the table and sat in the chair beside mine.

I looked at the worn circle of plain white gold on my left hand. "My first husband, Tim. We had a big discussion about this before he died…about me taking off my wedding ring. I told him I wouldn't, even if I lived without him for a hundred years, and he said *fine!* In just that tone of voice, I might add, but he made me promise to at least put it on my right hand so that I could make room for someone else in my heart. I promised him I would do that, but I never have. At least, not yet."

What had I just done? I stopped abruptly. I'd never told that story to anyone. Greg had hated that I wouldn't take the ring off, even though I'd worn the narrow circlet of blue stones he gave me on the same finger. Like any other narcissist, he couldn't fathom that my life with Tim had nothing to do with him.

It took me months to realize I'd not only written about narcissists in the Mayhem books, I'd married one.

"I'm sorry," I said into the quiet that followed my confession. "I don't know what made me tell that."

"It's a wonderful piece of your life," said Rose. "Not happy, I'm sure, but beautiful nonetheless. When our marriage was on the last little toe of its last leg, I kept my ring on, because to have taken it off would have meant giving up."

"I pawned mine." Sadie shrugged. "He wasn't good about child support and it was a pretty nice ring. It bought groceries for that week."

Cari looked unconvincingly mournful. "It must be admitted that I have yet to have gotten a wedding ring, much to my mother's dismay. I am pushing thirty, you know, and have been since my twentieth birthday. She's almost certain there's no turning back for me at this late date."

"That's only because you won't let me put highlights in your hair." Dallas raised her mug in admonition. "If you'd just let me add some burgundy to that dark brown, you'd be a shoo-in for a wedding ring."

Cari huffed. "As if I'd sell myself so cheaply."

Dallas grinned. "It's not cheap. I charge by the foil."

I laughed with the rest of them, and before we left, I made an appointment with her to get my hair trimmed on Tuesday. No harm in staying a few more days.

The Burl felt empty, but comfortably so. I was glad for that. I knew my proclivity for being alone might not always be healthy, but I was used to it. It was easy.

My mother's hair had been like mine, as far as I could tell from pictures, although she'd worn it longer than mine and wild around her shoulders. She had blonde streaks, kind of brassy, mixed into the brown. Aunt Lin said she was beautiful and had made her brother so happy. I didn't think I'd ever made anyone but Tim happy, but I did think I might get some highlights when I went to Lavender Park in a few days. Maybe some blonde, brassy ones.

"I know you're there and not answering. I'm going over to finalize some stuff with Tom and Dan Friday morning, then head for Harper Loch. If you want to try the recipe for those biscuits, I'll bring salmon on ice and we can cook that dinner. I'll even bring the cedar plank if we need it." Sam's voice, mellow and rich like any good attorney's should be, came across the speaker when I didn't answer the landline phone in the office on Thursday afternoon. Who still used landlines anyway? Besides Sam, I mean.

I picked up immediately, feeling a smile all over my face. "We do need one, although there is a really nice grill on the back deck." The snow had melted and central Michigan was mostly mud, too, but I didn't want to discourage Sam from coming. I would be glad to see him. I would finish the book today—it would be nice to have someone to celebrate that with…someone who knew Trilby.

It would be nice to see Sam for his own sake. And mine.

"That's good then. I'll see you at four-ish tomorrow."

I did finish the book, but just barely, which isn't very impressive when you figure I only needed a few hundred words to reach the end when I went to bed last night. Well, this morning. My sleeping hours were taking a hit here at the lake. Not that I wasn't getting plenty of sleep, but it was just at such odd times of the day and night.

I didn't feel very celebratory, if I'm honest about it. While I had one more Mayhem book to write, there was no going back from it being the last one. I hadn't read any of Trilby's preparation for *Mayhem on Monday*. I was nearly afraid to; what if the last Finlay Iverson novel was art imitating life? Finlay was an expert in poisons. He had many secrets of his own that had been slowly revealed in the series. What if Trilby had decided the series should end with Finlay sleeping calmly away on his couch?

I didn't think I could write it if that had been his choice. Finlay deserved better than that. His readers definitely did. For that matter, *I* deserved better than that.

When *Mayhem at the Fair* was finished, I closed its file to let it rest, then left the office, shutting the door behind me. Chloe looked concerned at this change in habit—I seldom closed doors, and she had a perfectly nice blanket in there—but I think she's still worried about my hair, too. I'm not sure she approves of its changes.

Dallas trimmed it on Tuesday, and did a good job, but it was the color that was amazing. I'd had highlights before, but never as many or as striking as the ones I had now. Chloe had barked at me when I came in the back door, not calming down until I laughed at her.

I'd brought three outfits when I came to the lake, thinking I'd be going home within a few days. It wasn't a problem, exactly, since I could do laundry here, but I felt like wearing something different … more different than my emergency outfit. Maybe even a sweater I hadn't spilled anything on. Not that I had many of those. Although I always wear an apron when I cook, just like Aunt Lin, I take it off when I eat. Big mistake.

"I'm going to Placer," I told Chloe. "I'll be back soon." I knew I'd seen a boutique there, although I couldn't remember its name.

"It's called DRAGONFLY," said Cari when I called her, "because the owner loves dragonflies. I know that's complicated, but I think you can remember it."

“I think pastors aren’t supposed to be smartasses,” I said mildly.

“If you think that, you haven’t known enough of us.”

Well, there was that. But if many of them were like her, I’d obviously been missing out.

“Is there anywhere else I should go when I go to town?”

“You’re going to Placer, not to ‘town.’ Willoughby, the county seat is ‘town.’ However, there’s a bulk foods store just ten minutes away from both the lake and from Placer. They have all kinds of spices and flour and different things most of us never use. If you’re one of those who does …”

“I am,” I interrupted. “Where is it?”

She gave me the directions to Squirrel Creek, which I didn’t understand a word of, and promised to come for lunch again soon. “I am a wonderful pastor,” she said modestly, “but I gave up cooking for it. I couldn’t possibly manage both.”

The Dragonfly was lovely. I seldom spent money on clothes, and the ones I did buy usually arrived in the security office of my apartment building in dusty parcels bearing the familiar curved-arrow logo of an online retailer.

Since I usually bought the same brands and styles, they almost always fit. The exception to that had been the purchase of the swimsuit I'd bought for the girlfriends trip when I turned fifty, when the ordered item had arrived the day we were leaving and would have fit a five-year-old child instead of a grown woman who fell somewhere between a size ten and a twelve—depending on how much baking I'd done.

The pretty boutique in the middle of one of Placer's three downtown blocks had a *lot* of things in my size, and I think I liked them all. When I left the store and the conversation with owner Maxine Greenway, I had enough clothing to spend the rest of the winter at Harper Loch. If I wanted to, which of course I—no, I'm not even going there. Who am I trying to convince by constantly bringing it up, anyway?

I hurried through the small supermarket, disappointed because their cheese selection wasn't as good as the one at the mercantile. Whether I wanted to go to a store in the middle of fallow cornfields or not, I was going to head for Squirrel Creek.

When I bought gas, I also bought six carved wooden roses from a man sitting patiently in a booth inside the convenience store with his wares in a woven basket by his side. "He's my Uncle Henry," said the woman at the cash register whose name tag invited me to call Adrian. "He has autism and is non-verbal, but he carves beautifully and understands what you say to him."

I nodded, appreciating the explanation. “Do I pay him or you for the roses?”

“Him, and he won’t take tips.” She smiled. “He can be very independent even in his silence.”

“Does he have a sweet tooth?” I looked at the pastries inside a glass case. “The flowers give such pleasure I’d like to repay that.” I wasn’t kidding, either. The flowers were gorgeous.

His niece’s smile widened. “He has a soft spot for anything with caramel icing.”

“Me, too,” I said truthfully, and bought him an iced cinnamon roll. I bought me one, too, figuring I had room in the new clothes for at least that many calories.

He beamed his thanks when I gave him the little paper plate. When I told him how many flowers I wanted, I asked if I could choose my own colors. He shook his head. “Okay,” I said, “I’ll take whichever ones you think, Mr. Henry.”

I thought reluctantly of Greg, who would have made fun of this silent artist. How could someone like him have been related to Trilby? How could I have married him without realizing who and what he truly was?

Mr. Henry gave me two white ones, two with soft blue wash on their petals, and two vividly dark blue ones, then added a full-blown peach-colored bloom. It didn’t match the others, but it was beautiful.

"Peach is for 'thank-you.' He has a list he printed off the internet that tells him what the colors mean. He appreciates your kindness." The cashier nodded at me. "So do I."

"Thank you both." Cheered by the flowers, the cinnamon roll, and the buyout of at least one sale rack in Dragonfly, I got into the car and asked Gladys to take me to the bulk foods store. I wasn't all that convinced Cari's directions wouldn't have me in the UP by suppertime.

The store reminded me of the Burl in that it had been added onto several times. The parking lot was so crowded that I wasn't sure I needed spices and cheese badly enough to brave packed aisles. However, manicotti is one of my favorite things to prepare and even though I'm no purist when it comes to cooking, I do have standards.

By the time I left Squirrel Creek nearly an hour later, my debit card was wailing in fear and a young Amish man helped carry my purchases to the car. I carried the two potted purple shamrocks myself. I knew I'd kill them in no time, but they were so pretty I couldn't pass them up.

I wondered, on the drive back to the lake, where I'd left Maggie North, because the person who'd just bought a whole bunch of stuff she didn't need certainly wasn't her. Right along with the thought, the sun touched the wedding ring on my left hand, and I almost stopped the car. Thankfully, I didn't, since there was a red pickup behind me.

It had been a long time since I'd felt Tim's presence, and I'm pragmatic enough to believe it's not him, but my yearning for him. Most of the time, the memories are sweet and not even painful, but every now and then, the longing is aching and sustained. Tim had driven a red pickup.

It was then that I thought maybe the sun glinting on my wedding ring was him reassuring me that things will be all right.

Is that what you meant, Trilby?

Chapter 7

I was so happy to see Sam, I felt as if my heart was going to burst through the front of the new coral sweater I was wearing with brown leggings. It hadn't been that long, but things felt so different here. I haven't been lonely, not for one minute, although I missed Trilby and our routine, but the aforementioned heart has expanded here. The

How does that even make sense? Sam and I have known each other for over thirty years and been friends for most of them. He's led me through more than one legal morass, including the one with Greg that broke me. In return, I've taught him to cook for one without having a week's worth of leftovers, listened to his beer-soaked regrets during his divorce, and served as mediator when he and Trilby went head-to-head over everything from chess to politics.

"You look great," he said, drawing back from the hug we'd just exchanged. That had been a surprise unto itself. I could count on one hand the times we'd hugged. Ever. Well, maybe two hands and a foot—it had been a lot of years, after all.

"So do you. You quit going to the scalper and found a real barber, didn't you?" His hair had gone from light brown to soft gray without experiencing either an awkward moment or, I swear, any loss at all.

“Maggie, it’s been two weeks since we’ve seen each other. I haven’t even had a haircut.”

Was that how long it had been? I’d met so many people in that time, been so many places, even though all of them were within thirty minutes of the lake on narrowish roads without lines on them. One or two of them hadn’t even been paved. Admittedly, I’d turned onto them by accident and Gladys had scolded me for my disobedience of her carefully worded directions.

“Well, you look good anyway.” I took his coat and hung it on one of the mudroom hooks. “Have you been here?” He’d come to the back door, but so did everyone else.

“Yes.”

Oh, of course, he had. He’d known where keys were, and garage door remotes. He’d called Sunday afternoon to tell me trash and recycling pickup was every other Monday and I could pay the bill for it at the mercantile. He knew the hot and cold water handles were backward on the sink in the laundry room.

Sam wasn’t a wine guy, so I got him a beer and set out the pretzel bites and cheese I knew he loved. While he and I were both good with silent times and the ones that often fell between us were never uncomfortable ones, there was no silence to be had this day. We talked about his present cases, with careful avoidance of using any identifying names or places. I went on—and on—about Harper Loch and everyone I'd met here.

After spending some time reassuring Chloe that he'd always loved her best—which was patently untrue, his life is run by a Maine Coon cat named Wilbur bequeathed to him by a client—Sam asked about the book and if I'd started on the next one yet.

"It will be the last one. I'm not in a hurry."

He looked thoughtful, an expression that sat well on his face. "You know, Trilby wouldn't mind at all if you carried on the Mayhem series without him. You've written them for a long time anyway."

"I have, but I was only the backup singer—he always sang lead. I can't write in his voice if he's not here to share it."

Sam didn't argue the point. He'd known Trilby as well as I had. We used to call him Muskegon's very own pied piper. Although he never insisted on having his own way, it seemed that he always got it anyway, with no effort at all. I remembered Claire saying she thought they'd had marital occasions when she might be able to kill him, but she would never for a minute consider leaving him.

I'd seen him around other women, so I was sure I knew what she meant, but I also knew he'd only ever loved one—her. Fortunately for Trilby, she knew it, too.

"Then maybe it's time for you to do what he said." Sam finished his beer and got up to get another one. I liked that he felt comfortable where I was. While I have no interest in having a romantic relationship with a man—Greg cured me of those particular longings—it's true I miss…

Well, what? Exactly what is it I miss? I can't pinpoint it, except to say it's nice having a smooth baritone voice across the table. It's a warm feeling seeing those shirt sleeves rolled up to his elbows. It's how he always wore them—he said buttoned cuffs drove him crazy. I asked him once if those bunched-up sleeves inside his suit jacket weren't uncomfortable and he looked at me blankly, as if it had never occurred to him.

He has big hands, a few of his nails worn down because he plays guitar every day of his life and doesn't use a pick. "When all else fails," he said once, plucking at the strings of the Guild guitar that rested on a stand in Trilby's office, "music is respite."

Sam was right about the respite. I'd played the spinet Tim and I bought used nearly every day. At least until I couldn't anymore and respite had become a thing of the past.

With Sam here, I'm not conscious of the pocket of fear that goes along with thoughts of Greg's release from prison. I hate admitting that. I've taken care of myself for a long time, but I'm not nearly as good at it as I used to be. Before I learned more than I ever wanted to know about spousal abuse and rape by a known assailant.

We weren't married anymore during that last horrific act of violence, although Greg still considered conjugal rights to be rightfully his. He'd been able to walk into the condo without so much as a tap on its door. Years later, I still couldn't explain why I'd never changed its lock or even its access code.

I'd thought he was as through with me as I was with him. The last months of our marriage it had become obvious that he hadn't wanted me at all—I'd merely been a way to get to his brother and to lay claim to things he considered his. Neither of them ever told me what caused the enmity between them, but it had been dark and deep.

When he walked unhindered into the apartment that night, Greg made me play the "Moonlight Sonata," always a favorite. He stood there shifting a little pocket pistol from hand to hand while I played. I was somewhere in the middle when I stumbled over a note and he slammed the fallboard down on my hands. I screamed, shocked by the pain. Infuriated, he dragged me into the bedroom we'd shared and completed what he came to do, holding the gun so close to my face I could smell metal.

Before he left, I heard him trash the living room of the condo, damaging the piano beyond any possible repair. Just as he'd damaged me.

While the rape was ugly and violent, the purposeful breaking of my fingers was in some ways been even more of a violation. He knew how much I loved playing, and he hated it just that much, because he connected it to Tim.

Even the gun he used to keep me quiet was the one Tim bought for me when he first became ill and we were given no hope for recovery. He taught me how to load it, to use it, to store it. "To keep you safe when I'm gone," he whispered to quiet my protests and calm my fears. "I need for you to be safe."

Safe. Oh, God, Tim. Oh, God. Greg took the gun with him when he moved out, but I'd never missed it.

Sam was the one whose quiet presence and listening ears beside my hospital bed made me decide to press charges. His gentle touch on my swollen hands was the deciding factor.

As if he knew where my thoughts had taken me there in the kitchen of the Burl, Sam asked quietly, "Are you playing?"

"I am." I was proud of it, too. "I've become good friends with pain-relievers and I've lost a lot of what I once knew, but it's so good to have a piano to play again." I couldn't think of it as mine. It belonged to the

Burl, as at home in its alcove as the shimmering colored glass was in the transoms.

Snow wafted down outside the windows over the sink, and the trees in the woods behind the house were already lacy with it. It was the end of the first week of March, so snow wasn't a surprise in central Michigan, but it was unexpected. The kitchen had darkened as we sat and talked, and I hadn't even noticed.

"Will you play for me?"

The words stopped me in my quest to turn on lights, to move around and be active. To get dinner started so we wouldn't be eating at ten o'clock. We were going to cook together, right? I didn't like the idea of him driving back to Muskegon with the snow falling. Unlike me, he wasn't a born-and-bred Michigander, but I was pretty sure he'd learned as much about winter driving in Vermont as I had here. However, ice was everyone's enemy, and there'd been a lot of thawing in the past week; the refreezing could be lethal.

"What?" I stopped my whirling-dervish act to look at him.

"Will you play for me?" he repeated. His eyes, unlike the faded-denim color of mine, came closer to the bright blue I loved. They were smiling.

I knew for sure then, that in this house full of magical surprises, the guitar in the alcove was his, tuned down a step the way he always did. It might even be the one that used to sit in Trilby's office. It, too, had been a Guild. More secrets I should want to know the answers to, but somehow didn't. "I will," I said, "if you'll play along with me."

It was still snowing.

"I can do that."

We played for an hour—longer than my fingers were happy with, but my heart would have been willing to go on much longer.

Back in the kitchen, I put on an apron and handed him one.

The grill was buried in snow and we'd forgotten to soak the cedar anyway, so he was going to broil the salmon. I was going to cook wild rice and steam fresh broccoli. We'd make the biscuits together.

"You need to get a new piano for your apartment," he said.

I hesitated for a moment, standing at the stove. "The walls aren't that thick there. I'd disturb people."

"You have the drummer in a rock band across the hall from you who practices all hours of the day and night. I don't think disturbing people is an issue."

"Yeah, but Jax is such a *good* drummer and a nice kid besides. I never want to discourage him. Besides, he practices in the basement and it's soundproofed." He was also the only neighbor in the quadplex where I lived who I called by name. I looked at him sometimes and thought if I'd had a son, I'd want him to be like Jax.

Sam raised a questioning eyebrow, and I knew I wasn't fooling him the least little bit. "Okay," I said, "I really thought I'd never play again. My hands don't work as well as they did, so I was afraid. Typing is easy—I don't have to reach much for it. The piano's keyboard is more of a challenge." I stopped again, looking up at the transom. "This house, Sam. This house."

He didn't answer, and we worked together in companionable silence. Chloe came in, looked hopefully at Sam until he gave her a treat out of the glass jar I'd set near the sink, and retreated to the window seat in the dining alcove. I'd stacked thick books from the library into steps so she could get up there and keep an eye out for any unknown intruders who might be advancing on the ramparts.

"You spoil that dog," said Sam, who spent more on cat food than I did on rent.

"Hush." I scowled at him. "She doesn't know she's a dog. And I'm not the one who gave her a treat just for walking into the kitchen." I often did, but Sam didn't need to know that.

The dinner was wonderful—the biscuits recipe was a win—and we sat for a long time after we'd finished eating. We drank decaf and acted as if it tasted as good as the real thing. When I got up to let Chloe out before she went to bed, I was amazed at how much snow had fallen. “Will you spend the night?” I said, when Sam came and scooped a path for the little dachshund. “I really hate the idea of you driving back through this.”

He nodded. “If you don’t mind. I should have kept an eye on the weather but I didn’t.” He met my eyes as we stood on the deck with our arms crossed against the cold and waited for Chloe to make her rounds. The little dachshund lifted her short legs out of the snow with disdainful exaggeration as she sought the perfect spot. “Truth is, I didn’t want to. I wanted to see you, to make sure you’re all right.”

I think I’m more all right than I’ve been in years, which I feel bad thinking so close to the time of Trilby’s dying, but I also know about honeymoon periods. I understand that I’m enthralled by the newness of the Burl specifically and Harper Loch in general, but I would tire of its smallness soon enough if I stayed. I’d mind having to drive a half hour to find the ingredients I want for a recipe that falls outside the norm of rural central Michigan. I’d miss Muskegon’s library and its parks and going to the Black Dog with Ellie. I’d miss Ellie, too, and Sam.

I had to admit, though, that it was fun seeing them here. I’d loved discovering Placer with Ellie, and Sam fit into this house as if he belonged here.

Maybe he did.

"So, tell me about the Burl," I requested. "My mind's been busy enough that it's kept my curiosity on the back burner. But you know this house, the lake, some of the people here. How is it that in all the years we've known each other, you've never mentioned Harper Loch?"

"We've known each other, but everything revolved around Trilby. You were his assistant, I was his lawyer, and we both loved him. Although you and I saw each other enough that we became friends, we leaned more toward just being acquaintances. Sometimes it was strictly professional, too. I was your lawyer. You helped my office staff if they were swamped."

I was unexpectedly hurt by being thought of as a mere acquaintance, but he was right. I frowned at him. "You're not answering my question." Realizing I sounded grumpy and he couldn't possibly know why, I stretched my hand across the table. "Hello. My name's Maggie North. I'd like to be friends."

When he took my hand, I understood what I'd read in romance novels about frissons—isn't that a cool word?—of feeling going right up my arm. I'd read a few where that particular shudder of feeling was an open invitation into bed. That wasn't happening, but still … a frisson is a frisson and I was going to enjoy it. And remember it.

If I ever write a book on my own, I will use the word *frisson.*

"Sam Eldridge," he said solemnly. "Son of Annabelle Newland."

It took a few seconds for that to sink in. Several. "Seriously?"

"Yes. My father was her first husband. He died in Vietnam shortly after I was born. Mom would have loved to have gone back to Canada, but her family had pretty much cut her off when she married an American GI from Vermont. She met my stepfather, Harp, during a snowstorm that had them laid over at the airport in Burlington when I was in high school. They got married before my senior year. Mom was willing to stay in Vermont for me to finish, but I was okay with moving here as long as I was allowed to play basketball. I got along with his kids—Cari's dad is my age and his sisters are older. Mom befriended Claire when she came with Trilby to the lake. They sat and spoke in French by the hour."

Something clicked, a vague memory. "Did Claire call her Belle? And did they travel together sometimes?"

He nodded. "Trilby and Harp were friends, too. They'd known each other since college, and they fished together here, in New England, and in Muskegon. A few times in Canada."

"Was Harp part of the family who founded this lake?"

He laughed. "Yes, several generations back, I think, but he was called that because he played the harp. His real name was Constantine, and he said Harp was a whole lot easier."

Finlay played the harp. Trilby had never mentioned why. I hadn't cared to ask when he was alive—why would I care now? It was no one's business anyway, and never had been.

"I don't know why he didn't talk about things," said Sam, and I wondered if he'd read my mind. Something in his face told me he had.

"I'm not the only one lacking curiosity then."

He shook his head. "He helped get me through law school. Even when Harp would have helped more than he did, Trilby said he was counting on using me, so he wanted to help."

He'd done the same for me. I hadn't gone to college, but he'd kept me alive after Tim died by professing to need me. Years later, he'd kept me alive again simply by being there and giving me work to do whether I wanted it or not; he knew I was as invested in Finlay Iverson as he was. He'd paid me much better than most assistants and ghost writers I knew, contributed to my 401K, and kept me in health insurance besides.

He'd been nearly as broken as I was when Greg hurt me. I don't think he ever quite forgave himself for introducing us, but one thing the brothers had in common was their charm. Even if he'd tried to stop me from entering into a relationship with Greg, he couldn't have.

"Was the Burl your stepfather's house?" That was hard for me to imagine. It felt like a woman's house. Cari had said it was theirs together, I thought, but had Harp owned it first? Had he put in the transoms that brightened the world every time I looked at them?

"They bought it together. Harp had one of the fishing shacks down at the end near the mercantile, and he also had a house on High Street in Placer where he and his first wife raised their family. Mom was willing to live in that house, but he knew she'd never feel at home there. Instead, they lived here after they bought it, although he kept the fishing shack for family use." Sam chuckled, shaking his head. "There was less of the Burl then, but every time one of them had a *why don't we do this?* moment, they built on. Mom did stained glass in the shed. Harp built another shed and they made really good maple syrup until it got to be too much for them and someone at the other end of the lake bought the business, shed and all. She made quilts—not good ones, but we all used them anyway. They just had a good time with everything they did. He already had plenty of money for his kids and grandkids and they separated everything so that everyone's interests were protected. The Newlands are great people. We were never made to feel like interlopers."

"Cari …"

He interrupted me with a chuckle. "Especially Cari. She's a sweetheart, isn't she?"

"But how did Trilby get the Burl, and why do I have it?" I was as mystified as ever.

"Mom was going to go back to Vermont after Harp died. She loved it here, but it was just too much house. I couldn't live here at the lake, because my business was in Muskegon. Harp's family live farther away—none of them had stayed in Placer. Oddly enough, Cari's folks settled in Vermont, in the house where Mom and I lived. She'd kept it for some reason—she said it must have been that she was saving it for Cari. She loved all Harp's grandkids, but she and Cari were kindred spirits."

He stopped for a beat, and I wondered if the memories were creating the kind of ache they often did in me.

But he went on almost immediately. "Mom didn't want the house to just sit here, so when Trilby offered to buy it, she sold it to him. She was here most of the time even then, with side trips to visit family, and Trilby and Claire came over, too. He called it the secret hideaway because no one except their kids knew about it. We weren't exactly told to keep it a secret, but we did anyway. It was fun for us, too, and its isolation was a godsend for family members who needed alone time.

When I was getting divorced, I spent a lot of time here."

"Its size overwhelms me." I'd thought it was about five times the size of the condo I'd had. That had been a serious undercalculation. It was closer to seven times.

"Mom used to say that, too, even as she and Harp were building something on. And then I'd be here and Harp's family would be here and the place would fill up and spill over. It's a happy place."

It was. I could feel that every day I spent in it. Maybe that's part of what feels too powerful to me. Although I was happy with Tim, that was the only time I had been that I remembered. Not that I'd been *un*happy, other than during the midlife traumatic mistake that was Greg Mathis, but life was just what it *was*.

"Let's go." Sam's voice interrupted my self-involved reverie.

I blinked at him. "Go where?"

"Go walking in the snow. It's stopped and the stars are even out. You have boots here, don't you? I have some in my car."

Until coming to the lake, I'd never walked at night—at least as an adult—unless I was walking *to* something. However, in my days here … or maybe I should say nights here … it was becoming a habit.

As I tugged on the new white puffer jacket I'd been unable to resist on Dragonfly's sale rack, I was stopped short by the realization that I'd dreaded darkness for several years now, and suddenly I was embracing it. *What gives, Maggie North?*

Take that, Greg Mathis.

Sam, his peacoat already buttoned, plucked the red cashmere scarf that had been Claire and Trilby's gift to me the Christmas before last off the counter and wrapped it around my neck, slowing with his hands on my shoulders and meeting my eyes.

"Warm enough?" His voice, always so smooth, sounded a little rough.

I was rather delighted with that roughness. "Yes."

We left Chloe sleeping and stepped out into the cold. Unlike the last time, this snow hadn't been wind-driven, so it was easy walking once we reached Enoch Trace. Jake and Emily were already out with their snowplows, and Sam and I weren't the only people taking advantage of the starlit night. We exchanged waves and calls of greeting with others, our voices muffled and ringing at the same time as they bounced off the water.

"I think I'll stay here for a few more weeks." I wasn't even sure when the decision had become final. Maybe somewhere between the Burl and the Bee. We'd walked all the way around the lake, our conversation desultory. When my foot had slipped on a piece of ice, Sam caught my hand and held it the rest of the way.

I wished we weren't wearing gloves—I'd have enjoyed the touch of his skin on mine. But I was being ridiculous. I was fifty-two and I'd left that kind of longing far behind me. Hadn't I?

"Really?"

I frowned at him. "Was that amusement I heard in your voice?"

"Might have been." He let go of my hand and put his arm around my shoulders as we began the trudge up the now-plowed driveway of the Burl. "Because I'm glad. I think this is a great place for you to find what's missing."

"Trilby's what's missing." Sadness, for the first time since I'd come here, became a suffocating cloak. I had to concentrate on breathing.

"I know. But he's not. He made sure you had this house, didn't he? That computer in the office wasn't my mother's. That room wasn't even an office. Although I hate the way he died—everyone who loved him hates it—he took care of us before he did it just the way he did when he was living."

"You, too?" I took off my coat and boots in the mudroom, hanging onto his arm rather than sitting on the bench to remove the boots.

"Me, too. That's why the guitar is in there with the piano. That's why Harp's fishing shack belongs to me now. Trilby bought it from Harp's family to leave to me so I'd always have the lake." He held up his hands, palms out. "Please don't send me there to spend the night. It hasn't been opened since last summer."

I laughed. He was right. Trilby is still with us in spirit, guiding us in the ways he thinks we should go. The thing with that is, even though his machinations often led to much eyerolling and pleas to "just leave it alone," he was usually right.

"So," said Sam, when we were sitting in front of the fire with our stockinged feet on a hassock in front of both our chairs, "what are you going to do for the next couple of weeks?"

"Explore. Get going on the last Mayhem book. Maybe figure out where I'm going. In life, I mean." I sipped from the hot chocolate Sam had prepared for us while I lit the fire. "It occurs to me that so far, my life isn't very relevant. I haven't done much with it."

It would have been nice if he'd offered up an instant argument, but he didn't. Instead he asked a question I didn't have even an inkling of an answer to. "What kind of relevancy are you looking for?"

Chapter 8

"Are you sure you don't mind? My mom said you helped Mr.Winterroad more than anyone even knew. I can pay you."

I'd thought I could resist the blue eyes behind Eamon Squires's black-rimmed glasses. Really, I had. I never overtipped him when he delivered my groceries—at least, not by much—and I'd stopped myself from calling him *honey* every time I wanted to. Which was often. But I was delighted he'd asked for a tutoring session on essay-writing.

"I don't mind at all," I said, pushing the back door wide so he could come in. "I think it's great that they have a writing club at school. We didn't have anything like that when I was a kid because it wasn't particularly cool. It was kind of like bowling, but we *did* have a bowling club." I'd become a decent bowler in the club, too, my only claim to athletic fame.

"It *was* great, until we got to the essays. I thought it would be a piece of cake, but Mrs. Laughlin, our sponsor, says fixing the grammar in a journal entry won't quite cut it. Thing is, I really liked that journal entry." He hung his coat on a hook and followed me into the kitchen.

"How many of you are coming?"

"Four. Will that be okay?" He looked anxious. "The others live in Placer. They'll be here pretty soon."

"Four's fine. Perfect."

He'd asked me himself after church rather than talking Sadie or his mother into doing it, which impressed me mightily. "Mrs. Laughlin's cool, really, but we're not getting it. She says being a mother and a librarian didn't teach her to think like high school people do. Could you just look at what we're doing and give us some advice?"

Those blue eyes had gotten me.

I'd talked to high school and college classes about writing many times over the years. Trilby had helped with the creation of several presentations, and they always went over well. I was usually asked back and I went gladly. But this was different. This was a bunch of kids sitting around the table in my kitchen. I had nachos ready for them, and cookies—molasses and snickerdoodles.

If I didn't do anything else during my time at the Burl, I was getting great use out of its kitchen.

And the piano.

And the computer in the office. I'd finished the revisions on *Mayhem at the Fair*—there'd been hardly any, and I thought the publisher was as reluctant to change anything of Trilby's as I had been. I hadn't been able to make myself open the blue binder containing the notes for *Mayhem on Monday;* instead, I'd been writing for myself, in my own voice. More like Paris Newland than Trilby Winterroad, but even more like Maggie North. It was crap, what I was writing, but … I loved it. I was in the office with Chloe and my coffee every morning before I even considered getting dressed.

Therefore, I'd had to think about where I'd put my laptop when Eamon asked about the tutoring session. I hadn't used it since I'd come here, but I wanted to be able to read their work on it.

Eamon looked at his phone when it chimed an incoming message. When he looked up, color was washing his cheeks. "Six."

I looked over from where I was getting glasses out of the cupboard. "What?"

"Not four. Six. Will that still be okay? If it's not, I can tell them that. They had plenty of time to get word to me before this." He grinned. "Of course, one of them's Mrs. Laughlin. I might be scared to tell her she can't come."

My phone dinged then, and I read my own message from Sadie. "Yep," I said, pleased Placer's librarian had sent me a last-minute request to attend. I grinned back at Eamon. "Do you think she'll give us any trouble?"

"She might. She's pretty fearless."

He helped me add leaves to the table and brought three more chairs in from the mudroom. By the time we were finished, the others had arrived.

I haven't spent a lot of time with teenagers since I was one. I loved Ellie's kids and Trilby and Claire's grandkids, but my exposure to them was limited. I was nervous about this session, no matter how much I liked Eamon of the blue eyes, but it didn't take long to realize my anxiety was misplaced.

They were hilarious and smart and loud.

I never wanted children after losing Tim, which I admit was shortsighted on my part. Not that I think a woman has to be a mother to be complete, but it was something I wish I'd done. I was glad I didn't have babies with Greg, but a wee small voice inside wondered if I'd have been so susceptible to the life he offered if I'd managed to make a more complete one on my own.

Complete meaning inclusive of hilarity, smartness, and noise.

And these kids could write.

"I have suggested to them," said Sadie dryly, accepting the mug of coffee I handed her, "that writing for publication requires discipline. So far, they don't believe me."

I laughed. "I have always had that discipline," I admitted, "because I happened into writing by doing

Trilby's typing from high school on. But I think maybe it's overemphasized."

Their gleeful faces showed me I'd said the wrong thing. "Not overemphasized," I corrected hurriedly, "but sometimes it has the wrong place in the priorities list."

"List? My mom makes a to-do list every morning." One of the girls shook her head, her curly hair bouncing with the movement. "I don't think she has much fun with it."

"But having fun with it needs to be *on* that list," I insisted. "All your life you'll have responsibilities, and they're important. If writing is one of them, like it's been for me, it needs to be something you look forward to, not something you dread."

"I think it's fun," said the other girl present, the one Eamon called Jonesy. "But the spelling and using the right verb tenses, not so much. I'd just like it to flow without worrying about that, but we get graded on those things in school."

"But not on your journal, I'll bet." I hoped I was right about that. "So, tell me this. If you're going to read something, would you rather read something written without regard to spelling and grammar or would you rather read something that flows as well for the reader as for the writer? If you're only writing for yourself, I'm the first one to agree you don't have to dot all the i's or cross all the t's, but if you're hoping someone else is going to read it and enjoy it, you need to make it easy to enjoy."

"Yeah, not like on Facebook," said the boy named Cooper. "I gotta admit, reading social media posts is what convinced me it was important to know the difference between *your* and *you're*—you know, the one with an apostrophe and an *e*."

We all laughed then. Not only had most of us made that mistake, we were annoyed when someone else did.

"Can we do a writing sprint?" asked Eamon. "With a prompt, I mean? Will you do one with us? We all have our laptops."

I was surprised. I hadn't expected that. I think I assumed they'd sit quietly and absorb the pearls of wisdom that fell from between my experienced lips. No, that didn't sound right, did it? My lips had had precious little experience in recent years, but I had no intention of discussing that with the company I was in at the table. The thought almost made me laugh again. I was glad they wanted to include me, though.

"You'll know how much help we need if you get a look at what we do on demand," said Jonesy.

The closest I'd ever come to writing for public consumption using my own voice had been the Paris Newland books, and even in them, the tone of the prose had been peppered with sounds of Trilby and tuned to the middle school audience it had been created for.

Could I do this? They were going to want to read it, weren't they?

"Give Maggie a break," said Sadie. "She may not have counted on that when she agreed to talk to you."

"I didn't, but I'd like to do it." At least, I thought I would. "How do you find your prompt?"

"We take turns, but we'd like you to choose."

"Okay." I looked at the transom over the window at the sink. "How about *pieces of blue?* Take it any direction you like. How long do we write?"

"Thirty minutes," said Sadie, "and if you have to go to the bathroom or get a drink somewhere in the middle of it, that's your tough luck."

I understood her purpose in saying that when three of the kids got to their feet, asking directions to the facilities. I couldn't believe they used the word *facilities,* but I was completely charmed by it.

They all ended up going, and Sadie and I used the several minutes to talk about the writers' group and the possibility of me talking to the book club at the library and maybe volunteering sometimes whenever I was at the lake.

My volunteering had always consisted of writing checks. I wasn't sure how Sadie had accomplished me offering up my time in the three minutes it took for the kids to start reappearing at the table.

“This is a cool house,” said Cooper, “but I should have had a map. I took a wrong turn and ended up in a hall with a door at the end.”

“That goes to the quilt room,” I said, “and I haven’t really looked yet. I stuck my head in, but it was dark and rainy outside and I couldn’t find the light switch. Cari says there’s a longarm quilting machine up there, but since I don’t quilt, I haven’t looked. It *is* a cool house, but it’s an adventure, too. That machine looked like some kind of monster in the darkness.”

“I love the windows,” said Jonesy. “The colored ones, I mean.”

“Me, too,” I agreed. *Pices of blue ... sapphires ... legends ...*

When everyone was reseated, with their cookie plates and glasses refilled, Sadie set the timer on her phone and started the sprint.

If a person, even one who’s written millions of words in her lifetime, has never done a writing sprint before, it’s a wonderful lesson in several ways. One of those ways is that people in their teens can think and write a lot faster than women in their fifties.

Their entries were all considerably longer than Sadie’s and mine. It also appeared that I had no imagination, at least compared to the five high-schoolers at the table, although I was grammatically superior by far. Big whoop.

A couple of them, including Eamon, had written complete essays.

They read their work aloud. "Mrs. Laughlin makes us do that," said Jonesy, "to see if it sounds as good to us as it looks." She made a face. "It usually doesn't."

"Yet," I said.

She looked startled. "What?"

"It will eventually, because instead of thinking it's not good at all, you'll hear the holes where you need to put in a thread of emotion or a surprising laugh. And you'll know where the sentences are too long because you have to take a breath in the middle or they're too short because they feel chunky." I gestured toward the windows over the sink. "It's like the pieces of glass in the transoms. You'll be reading along and there'll be something that doesn't belong."

"Really?"

"Really." I laughed then. "But you won't want to take out any of your pieces of glass because you love them so much."

They laughed along with me, but they got it. What a great feeling it was for all of us, that we understood that thing.

I read mine aloud, too, because they insisted on hearing it. It wasn't an essay at all, but the beginning of … something else; I wasn't sure what. I'd gotten stuck on the sapphires. The kids all laughed when I had a sentence that was so long I pretended I was gasping when I reached the period.

"Is that part of a book?" asked Cooper. "It sounds like it should be."

"Yeah." Eamon nodded. "I'd like to read more of it."

Find your own voice.

The words in Trilby's note became a silent part of the conversation. I couldn't unhear them.

Every time I'd stepped outside my carefully planned path, though, it hadn't worked out. I'd thrown all emotional caution to the proverbial wind and loved Tim with everything that I was only to lose him. Years later, when I'd decided it was time to try again with Greg Mathis, my life had exploded into shards of bitterness and hurt.

I'd been Trilby's ghost writer and I was good at it. I'd loved writing the books even though the stories hadn't been mine. But I hadn't been attached to the middle grade books under Paris Newland's name. I'd been relieved when the kids in the Lunchroom Mysteries went to high school and the series ended.

The voice had been, as I've said before, very nearly my own, but without the addition of my heart. I understood and remembered from the days of those high school essays that in a perfect world, heart and voice needed to be together when it came to storytelling. I'd borrowed Trilby's heart when I wrote the Lunchroom Mysteries.

But Trilby was gone. I had to find my own voice, as he'd said, both to write and to live, and I needed to put my heart into it, too.

I read the next sprint creation, Jonesy's, and understood that the tutoring session was teaching me more than it was them. It was all voice. And heart.

That Sunday, the music wouldn't cue up at church. We had to take our seats accompanied by the liturgist—it was Jake Crossley in March—telling us we didn't need music to know which pew we always sat in. He said good morning and read the announcements from the bulletin, offered opening prayer and said the first song was "When We All Get to Heaven."

"We'll just have to sing *a cappella*," he added, when Flynn, the audio-visual volunteer, announced nothing was working and he needed to go outside so he could swear aloud like normal people.

"Maggie," said Cari, in her best come-to-Jesus voice, "would you play for us today? We're not nearly good enough for *a cappella*. Plus if everyone hears Flynn swearing, they'll think I've failed as a pastor. We can't have that, can we?"

I was both horrified and eager. "I haven't warmed up," I warned, getting to my feet anyway. "My fingers will be stiff and I'll sound like a five-year-old on her third lesson in."

"Better than we'd sound without you," Cari maintained, beaming at me.

She looked a little too happy, and I wondered for a moment if I was being manipulated. Gently, of course. But surely a woman of God wouldn't take advantage of a parishioner within the walls of the church, would she?

Well, would she?

It didn't matter. I loved playing the old hymns. The more limber my fingers got and the louder the people in the pews sang, the more I enjoyed it. The closing song was "How Great Thou Art." Dallas Comerford's mother-in-law, Addie, who had advanced Alzheimer's, sang in such a true and beautiful alto that we all fell silent just to listen to her.

When she finished, to applause, a voice from the back requested "Will There Be Any Stars in My Crown?" and I played obediently, thinking of Uncle Bill. He loved the old Joel McCrea movie, *Stars in My Crown.*

I bought him the DVD of the movie, a theater-style popcorn maker, and a twelve-pack of beer for Christmas a few years ago. We spent Christmas afternoon in their Sedona living room, just the three of us. It was a wonderful day.

The combination of the sound of Addie Comerford's voice and the memory of that afternoon with my aunt and uncle had me blinking back tears.

Harper Loch was turning me into an inordinately mushy person, something I'd avoided most of my life—with time out allowed for anyone's performance of Leonard Cohen's "Hallelujah" and the ending of *It's a Wonderful Life*.

Another request followed that one, and then yet another. I got to my feet then, waving my hands to loosen the soreness that was cramping my fingers. After the benediction, it took a while to move away from the piano as members of the congregation gathered to thank me and tell me how much they'd enjoyed the music. My throat thickened until I could barely respond.

"So," said Cari, stopping me when I would have walked past her with a wave, "want to have lunch? I'm cooking."

"Okay." Good heavens, I sounded like a frog. I cleared my throat. "That would be good."

"I owe you for that wonderful music."

I stopped, looking at her until she met my eyes. "Why do I feel as if I've been taken for a ride, Preach?"

She grinned, her gaze moving past me. "That's a little harsh."

Before I could turn to see who she was looking at, Flynn Squires said, with a laugh in his voice, "Did I do it right, Cari?" He stepped around, extending his hand to me. "Great music, Maggie. Dallas told Cari her mother-in-law would be here this morning, and she loves to sing so much. She used to play the piano, too."

"I should have asked you first." Cari looked somewhat abashed. Not much, but a little. "But you made her day, Maggie—and not just hers. You were indeed a blessing to us all."

"You're forgiven," I said, feeling a little glow that came with the knowledge of having made someone so happy.

Later that day, though, sitting on the couch with Chloe and reading, I turned and looked out the front window, my eyes finding the lake beyond the trees. I felt the isolation of Harper Loch, missed seeing Ellie and Sam and Jax, and realized I'd forgotten something.

I'd forgotten that life on the lake wasn't real at all. It was just a piece of bright blue in the life I'd created for myself. Its glow, like the pleasure of making Addie Comerford happy, wouldn't last.

I needed to go home soon.

Chapter 9

March went out, as promised by the almanac, like a lamb. The bright blush of early spring was everywhere in rural Michigan. Wildflowers raised their heads cautiously and I paid the writers' group from the high school for two hours of their time on spring's first sunny day to help me clean out flower beds and plant annuals at the Burl. They were all better at it than I was, but I learned back in the days of helping Aunt Lin that it was a waste of time to resent my black thumb. I just planted things that no one could kill. Well, hardly anyone.

Chloe and I drove to Muskegon on the first Friday in April. It wasn't sunny as I took the back roads I insisted Gladys route us on for the trip home. Not that I've lost patience with highways, but I've developed an affection for byways without lines painted on them. The sky and the multiples shades of green in the surrounding countryside were promising even when the sun was in hiding.

I was anxious to get to my apartment, to sleep in a cozy eight hundred square feet instead of the thousands offered by the Burl. I'd be glad to see Jax, and wave to the other neighbors whom I barely knew. To lean hard to the right on the balcony so I could see Lake Michigan.

I was meeting Ellie and our two high school friends for dinner my first night back, to be followed by wine, conversation, and music at the Black Dog. I thought about taking an Uber to the restaurant and home from the Black Dog, but both places were close enough to walk to as long as the air stayed warm and the rain held off.

The apartment smelled stale, regardless of it being perfectly clean. Jax had put staple items in the refrigerator and turned on the icemaker, so I at least had sandwich materials and things to drink, but I wasn't that interested in them.

I turned on the computer, but I wasn't interested in that, either.

The ding of a text drew my attention. R U IN MUSKEGON? WANNA MEET ME FOR LUNCH?

It was Sam. My heartbeat did a ridiculous little dance, and I tapped in, TIME AND PLACE?

The phone rang then. "I'll pick you up," he said. "It's Friday so I'm not coming back to the office after lunch. Want to drive down to Grand Haven and see if it's waking up yet?"

"Sure." I loved all the lake towns on Michigan's west coast, especially when I was in good company.

I had time to change into capris and a sweater before Sam came. I even put on makeup. Jax offered to keep Chloe while I was gone, and I wondered if I should hire him to walk her and take care of her when I was busy now that I was back in town. He gave music lessons in addition to his band's increasing popularity, but we could probably work well with each other's schedules. I'd still have time for Wednesday coffee and the late-day walkers and the writing group from…

Oh, wait. I was home now, not on the lake.

I stepped onto my balcony, tilting to see the water. Below, Sam's car pulled in beside mine. When he got out, he looked up. How did he know I'd be out here? How overanxious could I look?

The thought crossed my mind that he wanted to talk about Greg. He'd gotten the date for his parole and wanted to tell me himself. He wanted to assure me that *everything would be all right*, even though it wasn't within his power to promise that. Yes, that was undoubtedly why he'd invited me to lunch on my first day back in town.

Dread made my bottom teeth hurt.

I took a deep breath, then a couple more. There was nothing I could do about it now. I waved at him. "Want me to go ahead and come down?" I called.

"Sure. Bring a jacket."

I laughed. "You forget, counselor, that I'm *from* Michigan. I know these things."

We exchanged a long hug before we got into the car for the drive to Grand Haven. The touristy town wasn't fully awake for spring yet, which was my favorite time to be there. While I loved my state's west coast and the town I lived in, my affection was in spite of the location's popularity, not because of it.

Sam shared nameless, timeless, unidentifiable situational information from his job. It never failed to fascinate me or lend interesting plot points to Finlay Iverson's most current adventure. "Oh, my goodness," I said, "what will I do with all this when the *Mayhem* series is finished?"

He parked in front of a lakeside diner. "You know, you could write more."

I shook my head, trying to dislodge the feeling of loss that came along with thoughts of the series coming to an end. "Not about Finlay. I feel like I'm pretending even now—his spirit and Trilby's are one and the same."

"So, maybe a new protagonist?"

He got out of the car without waiting for an answer, and I got out the other side, thinking. Did I even want to write? I'd been doing it, in essence, since I was sixteen. Was I tired of it? Had I ever even really *done* it, since Trilby had been the driving force all along? I had that secret file on a flash drive, the one where I was just me and no one else, but I didn't see it going anywhere beyond the limited scope of my imagination.

Sam dipped his head. "Maybe a middle-aged attorney with good hair?"

"Who happens to practice in Muskegon?"

He opened the door to the restaurant and I stepped inside, his hand at my back.

"Well, yes, since you know the area already, not to mention the meat of most of my cases."

Without knowing why, I shook my head again. "I want something different," I admitted. "I just don't know what." I thought this whole *different* thing was the fault of Harper Loch and its eighty-five residents, but it didn't seem quite fair to place all the blame there. Especially since I was home now and I still had no idea what I wanted.

We ate our lunch, still talking, and ordered coffee to go. At the nearby beach, we walked on the boardwalk, enjoying the two lighthouses, their bright red color lending cheerfulness to the somewhat blustery afternoon.

"He's out," said Sam, his arm resting around my shoulders. I was glad it was there.

Damn.

After an instant when I couldn't breathe, when I thought lightheadedness was going to have me diving off the boardwalk, and the stumble I hoped he didn't notice, I didn't know how to feel. It was like that first bewildering week after Trilby died, when I understood life was forever changed but not what to do about it. And now it was going to change again. And not for the better.

Fear wormed its way into my mind, making my mouth taste like metal, and a hard, painful lump form in the middle of my chest. When I first got to the lake and tried to play the piano, I'd get a pain in my fingers when I first touched the keys that reminded me of the night they'd been broken. I would not only taste metal, but smell it as well, as I recalled the gun, and I'd think the lump was never going to go away. It was going to sit there behind my breastbone until it absorbed every breath I had left.

I hated Greg Mathis for several things, none more than for that chunk of hurt he'd left in his wake and that he would probably bring back with him when he came to find me. Because I knew he would. And Sam probably wouldn't be there with his arm around my shoulders when he did.

He's out.

The Black Dog had gotten along fine without me. The red wine was still awful and Scott was still saying it was my taster that was off, not the wine. When Ellie and I admitted we hadn't gone to dinner as we'd planned because our friends couldn't make it, he brought an overfilled charcuterie board and laid it between us on our favorite high top table beside the window that gave us a view of the South Pierhead Light. "On me," he said. "Someone ordered it and didn't pick it up. It's been lying around the kitchen for three or four days."

"Should still be okay," said Ellie, grinning.

I couldn't be positive, but it seemed to me there was a little something-something passing between my friends. Scott's hand rested on the shoulder of Ellie's green sweater for just a second, and her grin—again, for just a second—was an out-and-out beam.

When he'd left the table, though, she frowned over at me. "What are you thinking?"

"That Harper Loch needs a lighthouse. I miss always being able to see one when I'm there."

"The things we take for granted." She honed in on the slices of summer sausage we always fought over, scooping at least two-thirds of them onto one of the plates Scott had left. "Have you made any decisions about the Burl? I hope you don't sell it right away. It's a great place to visit."

The idea of selling it made my stomach feel like lead. "I'm not going to," I said. I hadn't been firm about anything since Trilby died, but holding onto the beautifully misshapen house on the lake for a while was a good place to start. "Not yet, at least. I think it would be fun to go there on weekends in the summer. Maybe even a week now and then. There will be more people around then. More to do."

Ellie's eyebrows rose. "Like you suddenly want people around and things to do? Who are you and what have you done with my friend?"

I think maybe I'm finding her. The words leapt right into my mind unexpectedly, but I didn't say them. I was too surprised. I knew what she meant—when I was a kid, Aunt Lin had worried about my introversion to the extent that she'd had me tested to see if I was on the autism spectrum. I was not.

"I was just thinking," I said, "about when Aunt Lin had me tested. She wasn't relieved. Remember?"

Ellie nodded. "I do. You asked her why not, and my mom asked her why not. Her answer needs to be recorded in the little instruction book every parent needs."

Good heavens, Maggie, there's nothing wrong *with having autism, but I didn't want us treating you like a Chevy if all along you were a Ford. We'd be gumming up your engine in no time.*

I laughed. "Uncle Bill's the car guy, but Aunt Lin definitely has a way with a metaphor."

I was missing them more than usual. And there was something else about that, too. I wanted to show them my lake, give them a special room in the Burl that would always be theirs—I'd already picked out which one. I'd done that for Ellie—how could I do less for my only family? I knew Aunt Lin had worried about me since Trilby died.

She'd like Harper Loch. A long-time hand quilter, she'd love the longarm machine in the long room upstairs. Arthritis had robbed her fingers of the dexterity she'd always enjoyed, so her quilts were all pieced and quilted by machine these days.

A rowboat was in the garage, along with a plethora of fishing equipment. I could envision my uncle joining other fishermen at the liars' table in the back of the mercantile. The group met there regardless of the weather, drinking coffee and eating breakfast sandwiches and biscuits and gravy from the deli section.

I always went to Arizona to see my aunt and uncle, usually at Christmas and occasionally another time through the year. Maybe they'd like to come to Michigan this spring.

"Of course they would," said Ellie, and I realized I'd said the words aloud. "You'd have room for them at the lake."

"I'll ask them tomorrow."

"Why wait? They're on Mountain time, so it's not too late. My kids won't be able to be around for Easter, so, not that you've asked, but I'd be glad to come, too."

I felt excitement stirring, fluttering, and wondered—not for the first time recently—what was going on with me. One reason I lived in a small apartment was that I didn't encourage company to come and stay. Even the two times my aunt and uncle had come back to Muskegon, I got them a motel room that meant Aunt Lin wouldn't have to do anything at all while they were there.

Maybe she'd rather do things. Maybe she'd like feeling at home when she came to visit, and I had no doubt the Burl would welcome her and Uncle Bill just as it had me.

I looked at the calendar on my phone, then called.

"Is there a motel there?" Aunt Lin asked cautiously.

"No, but there are enough bedrooms in the Burl to be one, and you're going to love the kitchen." I thought of the quilt space. "There's another room I want to show you, too."

She laughed, the sound low and throaty and warm. "I'll have to medicate your uncle to get him on the plane."

"With some Captain Morgan?"

"Maybe. It's been known to work."

"I'll get your tickets." In business class, where I was certain they'd never sat. She'd insist on paying me back for them, but I'd lied about costs before, saying I hadn't kept the receipts. "You won't need a rental car."

"We'll get one anyway. I don't like to depend on you for everything."

"I'd like it if you *would* depend on me once in a while." I meant it, too. "I love you both. So does Ellie."

My aunt's voice went soft. "Back at the two of you, but you stay out of trouble, now."

I always had stayed out of trouble. Only much later did I realize they wouldn't have sent me away if I hadn't. They attended every single thing I was involved in at school. When I had my tonsils out when I was seven, Aunt Lin slept in my room at the hospital. At home, I woke in the middle of the night to see Uncle Bill sitting in a chair beside the bed. He gave me a drink and told me about when he played basketball in high school.

All these years later, I still enjoyed high school basketball, and I always thought of Uncle Bill when I watched it.

"You should ask Sam, too," Ellie said after I'd hung up, pouring the last of the awful red stuff into our glasses.

I looked at her, startled by the suggestion. Sam and I had never spent holidays together, although we exchanged proper, professional gifts at Christmas. I didn't even know how he celebrated, or *if* he did. I didn't know if he was seeing someone. Maybe I could invite him to dinner and tell him he could bring a *plus one*.

Or maybe I could send him a text wishing him HAPPY EASTER and just forget the whole thing.

"Have you started the last book yet?" asked Ellie.

I shook my head. "Haven't so much as opened the binder with the notes in it. Fortunately, there's no hurry." There actually *was* a hurry—the publisher had offered one deadline and Miki had held them off, but that would only give me so much grace time.

"Are you worried about what's in it?"

"A little." *A lot.*

Ellie frowned at me. Her eyes, usually the color of rich milk chocolate, darkened. "Are you also worried about something else?"

"Of course not. I'm fine. Life's just wonky anymore, is all."

She snorted, which she could do better than anyone I'd ever known. "Honest to God, Mags, I feel like I'm pulling teeth here. Is something going on?"

He's out.

I'd only forgotten the words for a few minutes at a time since Sam told me, then they'd come back in a rush. I know Sam hadn't wanted that, but he understood that I needed to know.

Even after Greg went to prison, I looked over my shoulder every time I walked out the door. When I was home, I locked myself inside so firmly that I'd never have made it out if there was a fire. When the Covid pandemic hit, I was more relieved by sheltering in place than annoyed.

But it got better. I've felt pretty safe for a long while now, especially at the lake in the house I was almost sure Greg Mathis hadn't known about. If he had, he'd have coveted it. He'd have complained about how easy everything was for Trilby.

I'd walked to the Black Dog with every intention of walking home, too, but the darkness gave me second thoughts. When Ellie offered … no … ordered me to share her Uber, I didn't argue. When I invited her to spend the night, she didn't argue then, either.

What had happened to feeling pretty safe?

One of the lights in the upstairs hallway was dark when we stepped out of the elevator at my apartment. I frowned up at the fixture, not because a burned-out bulb is usually a big deal but because maybe this time it was. And it was the one that lit the part of the hall that gave access to the door of my apartment. The one near Jax's door was still lit.

"Maggie?"

Ellie's voice sounded tremulous, which doesn't ever happen unless there are reptiles involved. I turned to look at her and followed her gaze to the cream-colored paneled door of my apartment.

The envelope taped to it, one of those bill-paying sized ones that seal themselves when you tear the strip of paper off the flap, was startlingly white against the mellow color of the door. Nothing broke the whiteness—no name, no return address, not even a wrinkle.

"Well," I said, "dang."

Although fear had made itself at home in my middle-aged psyche, there were limits to what I was going to be scared of. A crisp white envelope didn't even come close. Finlay Iverson might have touched the edge of the envelope gingerly for forensic reasons, but I wasn't Finlay. I peeled it off the door, annoyed because my fingers shook as surely as Ellie's voice had. Neither of us were trembly types, but there we were.

Going into the apartment felt creepy. Security was optimal here, even on the balcony. No one had gotten inside. Nothing was moved. The space still felt stuffy from the weeks of my absence.

But the envelope had been on the door. Someone had gotten that close. I would ask Jax about it, but if he'd seen or heard anything, he would have texted me. He was gone for the weekend anyway—his band was opening for a group from Chicago Jax admitted was "bigger, louder, and better-known."

Chloe was sound asleep in her bed, the same one she'd had at Trilby's. She sniffed when I stroked her head, but didn't wake.

Ellie and I got ready for bed, both of us wearing T-shirts and pajama pants that were faded beyond redemption—our favorite nightwear. We made our usual remarks about not being able to understand the lack of sex in our lives when we obviously dressed to attract, then we sat in opposite corners of the couch and drank hot chocolate laced with some medicinal rum.

I hadn't opened the envelope yet. I'd laid it on the kitchen counter and avoided looking at it. I hadn't even felt the bump in it that indicated there was something in it besides the threatening note I was trying hard not to envision.

Damn, Trilby, where's Finlay when I need him?

The thought made me smile, and when I explained to Ellie, she chuckled, too. "You just can't depend on a PI who watches *Andy Griffith* reruns and says things like *great Santa's beard*."

I nodded. "Remember in *Mayhem at Howard's* when Finlay's neighbor Howard Fenstermaker found something mysterious on his doorstep. He was afraid of it and left it there, using a different door to go into his house. He was curious, too, but mostly scared. I insisted to Trilby that curiosity would always win out over fear. Raised my voice and everything."

Ellie nodded. “I do remember that scene. What did Trilby say when you raised your voice?”

“He looked at me over his reading glasses and said, ‘Only if you’re a cat.’ I decided he was brilliant and I should just keep typing, so I did.”

I had to start on the last book. Trilby’s outlines and notes were so extensive that writing the story wasn’t usually hard. Finding his voice hadn’t been difficult when he was at the desk across the room from me, but I wasn’t sure about now.

The envelope lay there, mocking both my fear and my curiosity, and unlike Howard Fenstermaker, the curiosity won out.

The bump inside the paper was the slender circle of blue gemstones that had been my wedding ring when I married Greg. There was a note, too, with four upper-case letters in bold Times New Roman font.

MINE

Ellie frowned. “What happened to cutting letters out of magazines and creating the menacing note with them? No one wants to work anymore.”

I’m not sure how or why we found ourselves laughing so hard, but we did. Frankly, I didn’t get it. I had given the ring back to Greg as he walked out the door of the condominium our prenuptial agreement kept him from claiming. He’d said it was a family heirloom, so I wouldn't have felt right keeping it even if I'd wanted to.

When I had shown it to Trilby, asking if he remembered it, he frowned and shook his head. I hadn't known about the infamous family legend of the sapphires then. Truthfully, I came to doubt that the little stones were genuine. Like the marriage itself, the shine went off the wedding ring very quickly.

I put it back into the envelope, along with the one-word note, and laid it back on the counter. I would call the police in the morning, and I'd have to admit that I'd touched everything, but I'd learned it was good to have the call on record even if there was very little they could do with the information I offered. Finlay Iverson kept law enforcement apprised of things.

I had learned much from Finley.

They would probably tell me I should have called them tonight, but I was too tired, and I felt to the very depths of my soul that I wasn't in danger. Not yet.

He's out.

Chapter 10

I left Muskegon a few days later.

I looked at the blue binder that held Trilby's notes for *Mayhem on Monday*. I even opened it, but there were his handwritten notes between the lines of his typewritten ones, and I couldn't bear it. It hadn't been long enough.

Besides, Easter was coming soon, and so were my aunt and uncle and Ellie and Sam. I called the writers' group kids and they came to help me get ready. Between making beds, dusting, and them eating cookies as fast as I could bake them, we discussed noun-verb disagreement in writing. I was right when I explained it to them. Most of the time.

I joined the late-day walkers on Tuesday. We talked so much that we'd gone all the way around the lake twice before I realized it.

During the time I was in Muskegon, Amy Squires had experienced some Braxton-Hicks contractions and decided she'd just as soon skip labor and go straight to delivery, although she had a couple of months to go. The mercantile had a new supplier for meats and cheeses in the deli department and they were both cheaper and better. The blue cottage next door to the Bee was for sale. Two new pads had been poured for manufactured cottages on the second row. The lots were smaller there and an access road was needed, which was creating much discussion at the liars' table in the morning. Dallas had hired a nail technician who was taking appointments two days a week. Someone was doing some work on Lark Meadow, but that wasn't unusual. Although none of the walkers had ever seen anyone actually *stay* in the big house, it was always well kept.

"It's owned by the Campbell Foundation out of Grand Rapids, which is the political family who built it early in the twentieth century," Rose explained, "but as far as I know, no one ever does anything with it. It's the great Harper Loch mystery, along with a drowning that occurred long before most of us were here." She grinned over at me. "Then there's the story of how the Burl can be cobbled together in so many parts and directions and still be so beautiful."

"I'm thinking of putting a little basket of compasses on the table inside the front door," I said. "Everyone who comes to the back knows how to get around, but ones who use the front could easily end up in Ohio."

"Have you been in every room yet?" asked Cari.

"I think so, although I haven't spent time in most of them. It's overwhelming to go from an apartment with eight hundred square feet to a house that has about seven times that. And I'm pretty sure I'm underestimating its size." It was fun, too, I had to admit. "So, when do summer people start coming back to the lake?"

"Mostly May. A few in April." said Dallas. "Several of them winter in Florida, and they don't come back here to stay until it gets hot down there. Then there are the ones who rent their cottages out for weekends and the occasional week, and they'll start at the end of this month. Pam Whelan rents the other chair in Lavender Park when she comes back from Sebring, and we both stay busy through the summer months."

"Colby and I talk about building a coffee shop every year at this time," said Rose. "We have room on the property, but we never get to it."

I loved that idea. It made me wish I had entrepreneurial leanings. Maybe Scott would want to open a satellite Black Dog location, although I hoped he wouldn't want to sell that dreadful red wine here.

"We all talk about development here," said Emily, "saying *wouldn't this or that be a good idea?* But then we realize it would change things. We might grow in a direction the full timers couldn't live with, and we're selfish enough not to want that to happen."

I frowned. Although there was diversity in the population of both the lake and nearby Placer, Emily's remark had sounded a little more … shall I say … conservative ... than I was comfortable hearing. I felt wonderfully welcome here, but was that because I was so completely white and not of the type to make waves?

She grinned at me. “I know what you’re thinking, and that’s my fault because of how I worded that little pearl of wisdom. The truth is that many lakes, even small ones, become exclusive. People buy property on them, tear down the original structures, and build McMansions in their place. Property values escalate, to be sure, as does the tax base. There’s nothing *wrong* with that, but I’d hate to see it happen here.”

So would I.

“Harper Loch is a little oasis in the middle of a farming community, and even though we don’t have much to offer in the way of amenities, we are comfortably close to larger cities,” Sadie observed.

“We are protected by the Homeowner’s Association that’s been around as long as houses have been on the lake,” said Rose. “It’s old enough it’s not even *called* an HOA, but it’s still legal and binding. It’s not as onerous as most of them, but it does limit progress and development in ways not everyone likes. The bad thing is that when our kids grow up, they leave, but I think that happens everywhere, doesn’t it?”

“Of course, it does.” Haley Squires nodded. “It’s not as if there are jobs here. I’m happy Flynn and Amy have stayed in the area, but Eamon won’t.” She shrugged. “We don’t raise ’em to keep ’em.”

"Right." Emily laughed. "We raise 'em to support us in our dotage."

The laughter spread and rippled, and the warmth of it moved through me. The fear that had begun as a panorama across my mind with the envelope in Muskegon shrank to a hologram I could ignore. At least for now.

Uncle Bill and Aunt Lin flew into Grand Rapids the Wednesday before Easter and rented a car to come the rest of the way to Harper Loch. I offered—one more time—to pick them up or send a driver, a proposal that was met with a firm refusal. Again.

The suite at the back of the house upstairs was perfect for them. The bedroom was even painted Aunt Lin's favorite sage green. The bathroom had a walk-in shower complete with safety grab bars. Multipaned French doors led onto a balcony that jutted incongruently off the back of the house with a splendid view of the woods.

I hoped they would stay longer than the week they'd allotted for the visit, but they loved Sedona—they'd only been back to Michigan twice since they'd moved there. Uncle Bill played golf several times a week and Aunt Lin would miss her quilting group. I couldn't wait for her to see the longarm quilting machine that was just down the hall from their bedroom.

They looked like TV commercials for every product on aging that had hit the screen. Uncle Bill was as lanky at seventy-five as he'd been in high school. He still had all his hair—albeit it was white now, flopping over his forehead as sexily as it had when it was sun-streaked brown, and his stomach was still flat as a board—something my aunt and I both envied and resented. Aunt Lin's hair was gray, clipped into the same messy bun she'd worn most of my life. They were still in the mudroom when we all leaned into a long, tight group hug.

Other than Tim's, their love was the only one I'd ever counted on to the point of taking it for granted. They'd had to take care of me when my parents were killed—I understood the family and value system that decreed that—but they hadn't had to love me.

I could feel their age more than I could see it. Aunt Lin had been my height, but she was shorter than me now. As far as I could tell, Uncle Bill was still five inches over six feet, but there was a stoop to his shoulders I'd never noticed before.

"Show us this house," he requested when he'd chosen his mug at the station in the alcove and filled it from the Keurig. I was pleased when he picked out the cup I'd placed there with him in mind. "I'm pretty sure it's bigger than the school we graduated from. Don't you think, Linnie?"

"Pretty close," she agreed, "and guaranteed it has more bathrooms." She laughed, her green eyes sparkling. "Remember how excited we were when we made the storage room in the duplex your own little bathroom, Maggie?"

I did remember. I'd still had to go down the hall, and it was so small I carried my toiletries in a plastic tote because any storage space in the tiny room was necessarily reserved for towels and toilet paper. But it had a mirror and a lock on the door, things Aunt Lin insisted over Uncle Bill's objections I needed, and I cherished the ownership of it. It was Mine, complete with the tiny porthole window in the shower that my aunt had made with a bag of glass shards she'd found at a rummage sale. That window had been the beginning of my love affair with stained-glass and all shades of bright blue.

Aunt Lin looked up at the windows over the kitchen sink, smiling at the transoms. "Look at that," she said, meeting my gaze. "Someone made that for you, whether they knew it or not."

"The whole house feels that way."

We toured the Burl. As had happened every time I showed it to someone, I discovered new places. They loved their room, and Aunt Lin was enchanted by the balcony.

Then I showed her the quilt room.

Uncle Bill's arm hugged my shoulders as we watched her walk around the long, narrow space. "I'm going to take a nap," he said, speaking low next to my ear. "When your aunt comes to, you can tell her where I am or you can just leave her here by herself. She thinks she's died and gone to heaven."

I stretched way up to kiss his cheek, surprising both him and myself. "Nah. If you're not there, she knows it's not heaven. Enjoy your nap."

She was looking at the sewing machines on the counter beneath the long bank of windows. "A serger," she murmured, "an embroidery machine, and a regular machine. These were all here when you came?"

"Yes. Cari says her grandmother sewed and quilted and Harp, her husband, had this room built just for that. There's still fabric in the cupboards, patterns and notions in the drawers."

My aunt moved slowly around the room, opening doors and drawers and closing them, stroking her hand over the smooth countertop where the machines rested. On the other side of the room, a cutting table jutted out from the wall with a heavy dropleaf to enlarge it. A planning panel rolled like a barn door in front of still more storage.

"It's like a dreamhouse," Aunt Lin said. "Your office, the library, this room, that wonderful kitchen, the bedrooms."

"I think that's pretty much what it is. Sam said they married later, when their kids were almost grown and gone, and whenever one of them wanted to do something, they just did it. They could afford it, and I think they were surprised to have found each other at the point in their lives that they did. Making each other's dreams come true must have been a primary thing for them."

"Sam?"

"Annabelle Newland was his mother. Harp Newland was Cari's grandfather. They were friends with Trilby and Claire. It gets complicated."

Aunt Lin chuckled dryly. "Any family seems complicated to us, doesn't it?"

It did. Uncle Bill was an only child and my parents had been Aunt Lin's only relatives other than her parents, my grandparents. I remembered them, but not well—they'd both died when I was in elementary school. My mother hadn't had any family at all.

"The convoluted family relationships are like the house itself." I looked around the long room, thinking of the round library and the fact that every room in this big house had both beauty and comfort. Just like family. "Nothing matches. Every room is different. It has more architectural nuances than you can shake a stick at. And yet there's flow and sturdiness. You expect an old house to have places where wind whistles through or floors that creak, and this one doesn't."

She smiled at me, the expression warming. "My girl with the writer's soul."

The comment startled me. Is that what I had? Was that part of the reason I couldn't bear the idea of letting Finlay go? "Thank you," I said. "For letting me be your girl."

Her hand stroked my arm, a mother's touch. I leaned into it.

"You know," she said, "he promised us—Trilby did—when we moved to Arizona, that he'd take care of you. I think he did that, don't you?"

I gazed around the room again, charmed by it as I was with nearly every other place in the Burl. "Oh, definitely."

She looked satisfied. "But, you know what's good? What's good is that you'd have taken care of yourself anyway. You might not have had this big house, but you're like Mary Tyler Moore on her TV show. She had spunk, and so do you. You'd have found your own Harper Loch."

"I don't know. Greg—"

"Greg was an anomalous mistake, one you'll never make again."

"Aunt Lin, did you just use the word *anomalous*?"

She grinned at me. "I did. Where do you think you got that writer's soul from?" She peered through the windows. "It's getting dark already, isn't it? Were you going to go walking with your friends?"

I started to demur, to say I didn't need to do that on their first night here, but stopped myself in time. She wanted to sew, to learn the ins and outs of the longarm machine. She knew how to operate one—she'd taken a class in Arizona so she could use the one in the clubhouse in their community—but I didn't know if different models had distinctions that needed to be learned.

"I'd like to," I said. "Do you want to come?"

"Not tonight, but maybe tomorrow."

"Okay. You know where the kitchen is." Not that she'd need it. I was pretty sure she'd still be in this room when I came back. "I need to find Chloe. She's shy, but she needs to get acquainted with you."

"She'll be fine. Go enjoy your walk."

I left her then. When I walked past the open door of the room I'd given her and Uncle Bill, I could see him on the bed under the quilt sleeping soundly. His arm was outside the cover, curled around Chloe, who was also sleeping soundly.

In writing, I'd used the words *My heart was full* in dialogue. I wasn't sure I'd ever known, at least in the years since Tim died, exactly what that meant. Now, I did.

Chapter 11

Holy Week is a busy time. I knew that, of course, but since this was the first Easter season I'd attended church in a very long time, I guess I'd forgotten. I told Aunt Lin I didn't mind missing Maundy Thursday service and she gave me the Look. I've been told everyone who ever raised a child has mastered the Look, and I've come to believe it.

Uncle Bill managed to be rowing around the lake with Colby Harmon when it was time for the early evening service, so Aunt Lin and I left Chloe watching mournfully through the door as we walked to church, enjoying the fake-out warmth of the early April evening.

The service was short and simple, and by the time we left, my aunt had invited the Harmons, the Crossleys, and Sadie Laughlin to join us for Easter dinner. Cari was coming, too, as were Ellie and Sam.

I'd already ordered the ham from the mercantile, but I suspected my aunt would enjoy Squirrel Creek, so on Friday morning, we went there—the store would close at noon that day, so we went early. We were not alone in that. Inside of five minutes, she was talking about quilt patterns with two Amish ladies while I bought way more cheese than I needed. By the time it was cut, I was comparing lasagna recipes with a woman who was buying Lebanese bologna while looking over her shoulder fearfully.

"I just had the big healthy eating lecture from my doctor," she said, "and I'm convinced if no once sees me buy this, it won't really have any carbs in it."

"Good point," I said. "Let me keep watch."

The woman behind the counter asked in a stage whisper if the woman buying bologna wanted a plain brown wrapper, and before I knew it, the three of us were snickering like middle-schoolers talking about boys.

When we were back in the car, having bought far more than I'd intended, Aunt Lin opened the bag of homemade chocolates she hadn't been able to ignore and offered me one. "I've never seen you like this."

"Seen me like what?" I took what turned out to be an orange cream, let it melt in my mouth, and swallowed. I may have thought the word *orgasmic*, but I couldn't have said it to Aunt Lin. I was sure she understood all about it, but our conversations had just never gone that way. They had been more of the *read this and let me know if you have questions* variety.

"Oh, gosh," she said. "Your uncle can make me feel just like this."

Good grief. I'd always heard kids would make a liar out of you—I'd never heard it about seventy-three-year-old aunts.

She finished the rocking-her-world chocolate and smiled over at me. "I've never seen you this opened up. You've always been polite to everyone, but I wouldn't have expected the Maggie I knew to get into conversations in grocery stores or be at home in a big house on a lake in the middle of a place she's never been before. I've only seen you afraid after your parents died and after Greg Mathis did his damage. You've always been cautious to the extreme. Quiet to the extreme. Not unloving, but unaffectionate … yes, to the extreme." Tears blurred her eyes. "It makes me happy seeing you like this."

I'd known contentment often in the years since Tim died, but never to this extent. The eagerness to return home, the enthusiastic pleasure I was taking in people and places and silly things like homemade candy and plain brown wrappers—they were new to me. The nice thing was that I'd retained the good feelings when I went back to Muskegon, too, although homesickness for the lake had been instant and sustained for the entire time I spent in my apartment.

Even with the pleasure, though, Greg Mathis's release stays on my mind, made worse by the envelope on my apartment door. I woke sometimes at night being clutched at by fingers of dread. Chloe always creeps closer when I did, and I'd go back to sleep, soothed.

I have no doubt he'll discover I'm at the lake if he hasn't already, and I've become careful about locking everything, which irritates me but is necessary. I've also reacquainted myself with my gun, taking it to the shooting range in Muskegon to gain some comfort with the weapon. Although *comfort* is the wrong word. I don't like guns. Remembering that my own had been used as a threat against me didn't lessen that dislike, either.

The Burl had a sophisticated alarm system, too, which I suppose was common in large houses, even on Harper Loch.

"I'm happier than I've been since I was with Tim. I can't explain it, but I am." I sighed, starting the car. "I don't trust it to stay this way, but I'm enjoying it while it lasts."

I'd love to feel safe, too—I'd love it so much. However, I knew even if I did, it would only be an illusion. But I couldn't pass my fear onto Aunt Lin. It was something I needed to deal with on my own.

At the Good Friday service, as I played the prelude, I looked up in surprise when Sam came in and slid into the pew beside Aunt Lin. She kissed his cheek and Uncle Bill reached around her to shake his hand.

I missed a note, and Cari looked over in feigned annoyance. “It’s just my uncle, Maggie. Don’t get all butterfingered.”

The congregation laughed at my expense, and I felt color climbing up my cheeks. Back to middle school yet again. Sam grinned at me, and I smiled back.

I was so glad to see him, although his entrance and my wrong note had disturbed the quiet gathering of souls. Judging by the chuckles and forgiving smiles, they didn’t mind being distracted.

After the subdued service, Sam and Cari both walked back to the Burl with us. The clam chowder Uncle Bill made was waiting in the slow cooker, and the crusty bread I’d baked was still warm.

“I’m not eating,” said Sam, raising protesting hands when Aunt Lin set him a place at the table in the alcove. “No one expected me until Sunday. I’m going to stay in Harp’s fishing shack.”

I shook my head at him. “Oh, no, you are not. You said yourself no one had been in that shack since last fall. Your room’s ready for you.”

“Besides, you’ll hurt Bill’s feelings if you don’t eat. You know how tenderhearted he is.” Aunt Lin did such a poor job of looking pathetic that we all laughed.

“I’d just like to get clear on who’s related to whom.” Uncle Bill brought a beer for Sam. He was old school enough to not realize that nice women really do drink beer. We were old school enough to not let him know how wrong he was.

We opened a bottle of chardonnay and killed it as we ate and Sam and Cari related their many-branched family tree, including Trilby and Claire and their family's seats at the family table even though they weren't related to anyone except each other.

"So that's where Paris Newland came from. And you never knew it, Maggie?" Aunt Lin had enjoyed the stories much as I did. Although I was happy with our small family, it was interesting hearing about larger ones even if I couldn't keep relationships or dynamics straight.

"I knew Paris was for Claire, but nothing about Sam's family at all." I frowned across the table at him, somehow offended that we'd known each other for so long and yet in so many ways didn't know each other at all.

"We all became part of Trilby's"—Sam stopped, looking thoughtful—"posse, maybe? He was our common denominator. The center of the wheel." He drew imaginary spokes in the air. "We all knew each other, and he knew everything about all of us, but he was absolute in respecting privacy. He protected his, and he was no less careful of ours."

"It took me years to figure out that his public persona and the private person were exclusive of one another," I admitted. I'd known without him telling me that I was never to talk about his family or his home when I presented at writers' conferences or spoke to the press, but I hadn't thought it was odd. Even when he introduced me to Greg, I wasn't surprised that he had a much younger brother I'd had no idea existed. Their different last names had been confusing, but Greg said he'd wanted to keep his biological parents' name when the Winterroads adopted him and they'd granted him that choice.

Sam finished his chowder and looked sadly at the bowl. When Aunt Lin would have gotten up to refill it, I shook my head at her.

"He knows where it is. He can get more all by himself."

"He's company," she said, scandalized.

I met his gaze for a long instant as he got up with his empty bowl, and we smiled at the same time. I looked away long enough to wink at my aunt. "Not anymore."

He dipped refills for everyone while he was up, and got two more beers from the fridge. "You girls need more of that vinegar substitute?" he asked, pointing at the wine bottle.

I poured the rest into our glasses. "We're good." I thought Aunt Lin liked being called a girl. I did, too.

After dinner, Cari and I filled the dishwasher while Sam and Uncle Bill discussed basketball and Aunt Lin sneaked up the back stairs to the room she'd dubbed Heaven at the End of the Hall. "Don't forget," I called after her, "we have sunrise service on Sunday. Don't make us come and find you."

"I'm so glad you're at the lake," said Cari. "Not just because of the piano and how easy you are to convince I need to be invited here often, but because of what you've brought with you." She dipped her chin in the direction of the table, where comparisons were being drawn between Larry Bird and Magic Johnson. "Including our favorite uncles."

I was a little confused by what she said—other than my pretty blue car and Chloe, I didn't think I'd brought anything. The Burl—and Trilby Winterroad and Annabelle Newland—had done it all.

"You're welcoming," Cari explained. "You spend time with Sadie's writers from the library. You liven up coffee on Wednesdays. You've added energy to our evening walks. Harper Loch is so small that we literally do all know each other, and we're so glad to know you. You have, to use what I'm almost certain is a cliché, expanded our horizons."

I laughed. "It may be a cliché, but that's exactly what's happened to me, too."

Chapter 12

Sam and I walked Cari home, then made the trek around the lake by ourselves. When he reached for my hand, I curled my fingers into his and allowed myself to enjoy the sensation.

We stayed up late. Chloe deserted me to sleep with my aunt and uncle. I opened a window in my room just a little, enjoying the cool air. I knew I'd probably wake in the night and close it, and I hadn't left any ground level windows cracked open or even unlocked since returning from Muskegon, but for tonight with my most-loved people in the Burl, I felt safe. And still wallowing some in the happiness I'd felt when I ate candy in the car with Aunt Lin.

It wouldn't last. I'm a grownup—I knew that. But it felt so good, soft like the air that whispered in below the open sash of the window.

I thought of Sam's hand around mine as we walked around the lake, the warmth of him reaching parts of me that hadn't been awakened in so very long. Not that I'd been celibate all the time since Greg. I knew my girl parts still worked. But maybe I'm old enough or sexually conservative enough or maybe some things not enough, that I need more than physical release.

I lay wakeful and restless, thinking of the closeness shared each of the times Sam and I had been together since Trilby's passing and wondering what … well, just wondering. Would we go further in our experimental touching? So far, we were at the level of inexperienced high schoolers—just feeling our way. What was curious about it was its very lack of strangeness. I'd always thought I knew myself pretty well, and yet I'd known Sam Eldridge for thirty years and never felt anything but friendship. Mostly professional friendship, at that.

Or had I? It wasn't the first time I'd been unsure about that. I thought of those frissons of sensation I'd ignored.

I finally slept, but woke long before dawn. Not exactly rested, but wide awake nonetheless, I dressed in brown leggings and an oatmeal-colored sweater with a deep cowl collar and sleeves that stayed up when I pushed them to my elbows. After washing my face and brushing my teeth, I might have put on a little makeup.

In the kitchen, making a full pot of coffee instead of a single cup and setting out the ingredients for cinnamon rolls, I chuckled at my reflection in the window. I didn't think I'd ever in my life worn lipstick and mascara at four o'clock in the morning. Unless I hadn't taken it off the night before, which was a distinct possibility.

I was kneading the dough when Sam came into the kitchen. His hair was combed straight back and he had on glasses instead of contacts. I liked him in the dark frames. "You look very professor-ish. You should wear them when you teach at the community college."

"I couldn't do that. We play basketball after class. Is there coffee?"

I nodded, turning the dough with a thump on the island's surface. Flour drifted up in a cloud that I was sure turned my darkened lashes an unattractive shade of powdery tan. "Will you top mine off?"

The dough became a ball in my hands, elastic and smelling wonderful. Claire taught me to bake bread one summer when Trilby worked at home and I spent a lot of time at their farmhouse. At Christmastime that year, when I was still broken and she was suffering the effects of chemo, we made sweetened dough and I mastered cinnamon rolls. I loved making bread, but the desserty rolls held my heart. Claire's, too.

Trilby stayed home with her the last six months of her life. Early one Tuesday morning, before I'd even gotten up, he called me and asked me to come to the farm. "Claire wants cinnamon rolls."

So, I'd driven halfway across the state, taking flour and yeast and cinnamon and cream cheese with me in case there wasn't any at their house, and made cinnamon rolls. She was only able to eat little pieces of them, but they made her happy. Trilby's family sat at the kitchen table and ate the rest of them. I made a couple of batches. As evening fell, I went into the room where Trilby sat beside the love of his life. He was sleeping … her hand in his. I bent and kissed her cheek and we whispered promises and soft laughter. We both knew I wouldn't see her again.

Remembering the bittersweet farewell, I set the dough to rise, noting the time, and walked around the island to sit beside Sam. "I'm glad you came early."

"Me, too."

We talked about plans for the day. "I thought I'd see what kind of shape the fishing shack is in," he said. "Sometimes critters get in there during the winter months and don't clean up after themselves. No one in the family ice fishes, but that doesn't mean no one ever uses it. It's been the venue for more than one unapproved party. Trilby's grandboys had to paint the whole interior a couple of years ago because they and their friends left it such a mess. Their fathers helped them only to make up for not having been caught the times they were the ones there without permission."

"I'll go with you," I offered. "I've never been in a fishing shack. Aunt Lin's going to spend the day in the quilt room and Uncle Bill's going to an auction with Colby and Jake, so I'm free to go along and get in your way."

"It can be our second date."

I frowned. "I don't remember the first one."

"It was the last time I was here, when we fixed dinner together." He turned on the barstool, grasping the back of my seat lightly and turning me at the same time. Our knees bumped, and I thought abstractedly that I needed to move the stools farther apart.

Except, of course, that I liked the feel of his knees against mine. The touch was gentle, more of a rub than an actual bump. He was wearing black sweatpants and a University of Michigan sweatshirt. He'd gone to law school there. I wasn't sure where he'd gone to college.

"Did you go to college there or in Vermont?" I asked, pointing at the shirt.

"University of Michigan start to finish. Thanks to Trilby and Harp and umpiring Little League ballgames in the summer."

He'd had scholarships, too—I remembered that for some reason—and done work-study at least part of the time.

"Tell me about your wife." I didn't know where the words had come from, and I'd have given most anything to take them back. For someone who didn't want anyone minding her business, I evidently didn't have any problem with bluntly minding his.

Sam shrugged. "She married what she thought my future was going to be and I married how she'd grown up. She expected that because I was interested in politics, I would enter them. Her family was straight from the 1950s era of family television and, as much as I loved our convoluted family, hers was what I wanted. Neither of us would give even an inch."

"Where is she now?"

"Married to a state senator in Illinois. She calls sometimes." The words sounded hollow, and I had the feeling he wished she wouldn't.

"Is she happy?" I asked because it was worry that was shadowing the blue of his eyes. Envy of his having loved her scratched at the edges of my mind and I hated it. I'd seen what jealousy could do, how Greg had never been able to forgive that I had loved another man before him.

I continued to love Tim even as I'd also loved Greg. Or thought I did. While I would never forgive him, would never think his name without dread, I suppose in a way I had done him a disservice, too. I never should have married him when I didn't have a whole heart to offer. I'd told him that, saying I didn't know if I'd ever be fully invested in our marriage, so it hadn't been under false pretenses. He'd said he understood. He'd been willing to give it our best shot.

But I still shouldn't have married him. I shouldn't have. For so many reasons that I wasn't sure how much that one counted, but still …

"I don't think she is. But we fell out of love with each other long before we separated. We didn't part as friends the way you'd always like to. There's no real emotional attachment between us, but I still wish her the best." He looked away, gazing toward where the sky was brightening the colors in the transom. "She used to threaten suicide, which was exhausting, and I guess I still worry that she'll actually do it. That's why I don't urge her not to call. The thing is, do I worry about it for her sake or for mine?"

I thought of Greg, remembering all the times during these past years that I'd hoped someone would contact me and tell me he'd died in jail. I didn't wish violence on him, not really—food poisoning would work, or maybe dying in his sleep or falling and hitting his head. Really hard against concrete. I would even pay for his funeral as long as no one asked me to plan or attend it.

As far as I knew, Trilby's kids and grandkids were his only family, and they hardly knew him.

"It wouldn't be your fault," I said now, laying my hands over Sam's. His fingers were longer and bigger than mine, and none of them were misshapen the way mine were. I traced the crooked wear on his guitar-playing fingernails.

He turned his hands and lifted mine. "I love that you play," he said. "Do they still hurt?"

"Sometimes, but it hurts more not to play."

"We need to find something out."

I knew what he meant before he let go of my fingers and drew me to him. I didn't object when I slipped off my stool or when he tilted my face up to his and kissed me with years' worth of wondering and searching. I didn't know how much of the wash of feeling and longing was his and how much was mine, but I did know the emotion flowed through me like Rapunzel's hair in drawings—long and silky and curving.

Emotion and something else. Longing and something else. He leaned back, just a little, meeting my eyes and smiling into them. "So, Maggie North, what's this you say?"

I shook my head, laughter rippling up and surprising me. "I didn't say anything."

He cupped my face in his hands—oh, the warmth. I didn't think I'd ever be cold again—and tilted his head for that firm, gentle mouth to take mine again. We were in our fifties, experienced kissers. I understood the jumping around inside and the skittery dance of my heartbeat. I understood the sudden sensitivity of my breasts, that I could feel their weight inside my bra. I got it, as he held me ever closer and deepened the kisses we shared, how precious this zero-dark-thirty time was. I understood the depths of the itch.

I dipped my head, laying it against the shoulder of his sweatshirt, then raised it again to have my turn at taking his lips and tasting. Like me, he'd brushed his teeth before coming to the kitchen, and he tasted of toothpaste and coffee and … oh, sweetness.

"Plundering," I murmured against his mouth.

He drew back again. "Huh?"

"I've written it," I explained. "We're plundering each other's lips."

"Nah. Plundering is stealing stuff so you have to go to court and I can get you thrown in jail or keep you out depending on how much you want to pay me."

I burst into laughter, knowing his integrity much too well to go for that one. "It's that, too, but when—"

"We're just deposing each other a little bit. Checking out witness reliability and all that. I think you're a fine material witness." He interrupted himself to kiss me again. I very nearly moaned with the pleasure of it. I held it back, but a whimper escaped, and he chuckled as he bent his head to kiss the hollow of my neck inside the soft cowl of my sweater. His breath was warm and fast, the feel of his lips on my skin some glorious word I hadn't figured out how to write yet.

"Yes, ma'am. A fine one."

What was he talking about? "A fine what?"

"Witness. Material."

"Oh."

"For when I go plundering."

We both plundered a little more then, until I got up, pushing him away with light hands on his shoulders. “Cinnamon rolls.”

“Oh, yeah.” But he gave me one more smacking kiss before subsiding. “I might have to plunder them when they’re done.”

“Kiss them?” I raised my eyebrows at him as went to get the bowl of doubled-in-size dough. “You’re going to kiss pastries?”

He came around the island, carrying his coffee mug, and pulled me into his side, the motion reminding me of his height. “If you make them, you bet.”

I heard Chloe’s tags jingling as she hurried down the stairs. “Will you let her out? It’s always urgent in the morning, and she’s had to come downstairs, so she’s really hustling.”

He opened the back door and the mudroom door, and the little dachshund sailed past both of us without so much as a yip of greeting. I watched through the window as she ran to her chosen spot at the edge of the woods and relieved herself.

A moment later, with her ears flapping as she ran, she scrambled toward the house and breakfast, stopping this time to let Sam assure her she was indeed the best dog in the world.

I have always loved mornings. Although I spend more time alone than is probably good for me, there is something about the solitude of the early hours that does, as the Psalm promises, restore my soul.

But for this early April morning on a little Michigan lake, I was glad not to be alone. And both my soul and my heart seemed to be thriving on restoration.

Easter Sunday was a long and enjoyable day. The Burl was its usual welcoming self, the food was wonderful, and so was the company. Ellie brought Scott with her at my behest, although she'd insisted there was nothing between them except a love for coffee and red wine that tasted like vinegar and food coloring.

After a huge dinner, some of us went walking, some went fishing, and some went back to the quilting room. Later in the afternoon, naps were taken and games were played. Cari and Uncle Bill argued about the lyrics of "Joshua Fit the Battle of Jericho" until Sam and I played it and everyone else sang it and we never did figure out who was right and who wasn't—we just went with whoever was loudest.

It was dark when people began to leave, taking foil-wrapped leftovers and half-bottles of wine to be shared in their own homes. Cari prayed everyone on their way, a process that nearly brought me to tears.

"I'm fifty-two," I said "and this is the best holiday I've ever had."

Everyone was gone except Cari, Sam, and my aunt and uncle, and we'd walked across Enoch Trace to stand at the shore of the lake. The moon was nearly full, lending silver light to the quiet water. The air was nighttime cool, but with the promise of spring in it.

"This is a beautiful place, Maggie." Aunt Lin's voice was hushed. "I'm so glad you have it, that Trilby took care of you in this way." She stood close to Uncle Bill, and for a moment, I couldn't speak at all. They'd loved and taken care of me all my life—was it hurtful to them that such a magnificent gift as the Burl had come from someone else?

"Me, too." I spoke quietly, too, neither trusting my voice or wanting to disturb the evening calm. "I'll never know why he left it to me, but I will be forever grateful." I cleared my throat, tried to speak, and cleared it again. "Just as I am grateful for you two becoming my parents and always wanting me to be your child. I love you both so much and I have to say it often to make up for all the times I haven't said it at all."

We didn't hug each other, standing there at the water's edge, but Uncle Bill grasped my fingers and squeezed gently. Aunt Lin's hand sculpted my cheek for just a moment of speaking silence.

Sam's arm came around me, surprising me because we'd made the tacit decision to keep our relationship changes—if that was what they were—to ourselves.

"I'm fifty-four," he said, "and it's the best one I've ever had, too."

I leaned into him, thinking about these people who were so very dear to me. I was so glad I'd learned to tell them. To show them.

Thanks, Trilby.

"It was a wonderful day," said Cari.

Sam put his free arm around her neck and pulled her to him, kissing the top of her head. I thought of what day it was and remembered the jubilance of the morning at church.

Jubilance, yes. Yes, indeed.

Chapter 13

I talked Aunt Lin and Uncle Bill into spending an extra two weeks on the pretext that it would allow her to finish the quilt I was absolutely certain she was making for me. Besides, he was spending as much time fishing as she was quilting. He'd also taken over walking Chloe and she was doing a fine job of pretending I didn't even exist.

Sam and I texted a lot. Sometimes we talked on the phone late at night. His jokes were as bad as Uncle Bill's, but slyer and more surprising, and I'd bury laughter in my pillow. Then he'd say "Goodnight, stars."

I'd whisper back, "Goodnight, air."

Thank you, Dr. Seuss, for lending tender words to a couple of grownups.

I would sleep so well then, with his voice still warm in my ear, the pillow holding the echoes of our shared laughter. It was a gentle time, a time when the tenuous faith that everything would be all right felt solid and true.

I knew I should be working on Trilby's last book, but I left the blue binder lying on a table in the office. It would still be there, I reasoned every morning, when I was ready. Then I would go fishing with Uncle Bill or to the quilt room with Aunt Lin. I would never be good at her art, but I was learning it, and she was a patient teacher. I regretted that I hadn't learned before—not so much because I liked quilting, but because of the time with Aunt Lin. It was what Cari called Wednesday coffee—manna for the soul.

Sometimes, though, I sat at the computer and wrote as Maggie North. I wasn't sure what I was writing, but it was fun. It kept the sense of dread at bay, the one that sometimes woke me trembling from an unremembered dream even if I'd gone to sleep with the sound of Sam's voice still in my ear.

Late on the second Friday night after Easter, Jax called after getting home from a gig, which he never did, to tell me the alarm system on our four-unit building had been compromised but that it would be repaired and all codes changed the following day. "Maybe it was kids," he said. "Probably out doing the spring fever thing. They didn't get into the building."

Neither of us believed it had been kids sowing their wild oats, not considering the vault-like security of our building, but I was glad he called me when the discovery was made instead of waiting until morning. I wasn't sure how to be prepared for what lay ahead, only that I needed to be. His effort to talk me off the ledge ended in laughter. Family, as I knew, didn't always require shared genes.

When we hung up, though, fear clutched at my stomach and tension overtook me to the extent that I got leg cramps. I walked through the downstairs of the Burl seeking release from both the pain and the dread that caused it, finally taking coffee into the office, sitting at the desk, and typing CHAPTER 1 on a new document.

That was how I started every book for Trilby. There was time for titles later, although I often knew ahead of time what they were, as I did now. His notes had to be … well, translated … for want of a better word, but they were linear, so sometimes I could type almost straight from them without any rearranging of puzzle pieces. He always had a careful outline, too, which oddly enough was harder for me to work from. We used to joke about me having to get over the need to correct his mistakes. He hadn't made many, but he was right—I did enjoy finding and correcting them. I'm not sure what that said about me.

I opened the blue binder and began, with great determination, to read Trilby Winterroad's last story.

Even sitting beside a window, I didn't notice daylight creeping into the little settlement on the lake. Uncle Bill and Chloe came down the back stairs, but I could barely hear them in the office. My cup disappeared from beside me and was replaced by another one, its contents steaming and fresh. Aunt Lin's hand rested briefly on my shoulder and I tilted my head toward it in greeting.

Sometime during those morning hours, I went to the bathroom and brushed my teeth and combed my hair. When Uncle Bill appeared at the door of the office, I looked up.

"Your aunt says lunch is ready. Do you want it in here?"

Lunch? Really? My stomach rumbled in response and I realized I hadn't had breakfast, had I? The thought made me laugh—I never willingly missed a meal. "No, I'm going to get dressed," I said, "and then I'll come to the kitchen. Don't wait for me."

But I had to drag myself away. I looked down at the computer after I'd stood, where CHAPTER 3 announced itself at the top of the page. I wasn't sure how I'd gotten that far. I was totally mesmerized by the story, by the things Trilby had written that I knew as well as I knew my own name weren't entirely fiction.

I almost sat down again, not wanting to leave the story, but I knew Aunt Lin would find me, armed with *the look* telling me there'd be no more shenanigans or meal-skipping.

This was how writing was after Greg attacked me, I remembered. Once I went back to work, I spent long hours in Trilby's office, using a speech recognition program until my hands had healed enough for me to use the keyboard. Jax, the only other tenant in our building at the time, was in his early twenties and new to Muskegon. He offered to drive me to work and pick me up afterward, even rearranging lessons with his drum students to accommodate my awkward schedule. Although I barely knew him then, I accepted the offer until I felt secure enough to walk or ride my bicycle again.

Eventually, life had achieved a new kind of normal. At least, until Trilby died.

Now, slipping back into my chair after lunch, it was as if he wasn't really gone at all. His voice was so apparent in the notes that I could almost hear it. I could see him pacing around the office in search of a way to finish a sentence. He had days where he wrote thousands of words and other days when he wrote a painstaking paragraph. It was how he'd written before handing the putting-it-on-paper part over to me.

As I read and wrote, I realized that much of what was in the blue binder had been written long before. Some of it was dated, which Trilby's work never was. In the notes, however, Finlay searched out a telephone booth and called a friend who had died in an earlier book. He didn't have his dog, Philco, who had appeared sometime near the middle of the series when he was found in a vintage refrigerator in an alley. He hadn't yet decided to curb his swearing at his friend Darby's request.

What really captured my attention, though, and kept me glued to my seat until my eyes were hot and dry with fatigue and the page on the screen was riddled with typos, was the story itself. From the very first page.

When someone died in his search for a fortune in sapphires.

My folks left the next morning. They asked me to come to Arizona to “help with some late spring cleaning,” but the last thing I wanted was for Greg Mathis to go through them to find me.

“Since when,” I asked, “do you do spring cleaning?” That would involve there actually being anything to clean, and there never was in Aunt Lin’s house. “Don’t worry about me. I will be fine. I’ll be there for Thanksgiving.”

They accepted that, albeit not happily, and Uncle Bill went over my gun for the second time since he’d gotten there, watching me load it, unload it, and lock it back in its vault. We took “one more walk” through all the locks on all the doors that opened into the Burl, the garage, and the shed. He checked the alarm system, alerting the sheriff’s office of his intent before doing so.

He looked into my face for a long time, as if memorizing it, and I found myself doing the same thing with his. He hadn’t had to love me, this man who’d married my aunt expecting a life of adventure and no children, but he had.

We hugged each other hard, there on the back stair landing on our way to the kitchen, where yet another stained-glass window there winked at us with rays of blue and gold and red.

"What will Chloe do when you're gone?" I asked, sounding a little breathy.

"She'll be glad to have her mom back. We told her to take care of you, and she takes her job seriously."

Aunt Lin was at the bottom of the stairs, her arms full of a sampler quilt whose colors reflected those in the landing window. "I brought the blocks from home, which I know you'd already figured out," she said.

We spread it out so I could see all the different patterns. It was breathtaking. When they were gone, I'd put it on my bed and maybe cry over it. But right then it was just one of those perfect moments that I keep locked away in a compartment behind my heart.

Their rental car pulled away with them waving energetically out the windows on both sides. I didn't fear, as I had sometimes done before, that I wouldn't see them again, but the house felt empty when I went back in. Chloe trotted ahead of me, stopping only long enough for me to pick up my cup and a plate of cookies. She led me straight to the office and settled onto her pillow.

I sipped coffee, ate an iced sugar cookie decorated with flowers created by dragging toothpicks through dots of pink and green, and opened the file, smiling at the page that appeared. CHAPTER 4. It was going so fast, this last book. I needed to slow down.

The writing in *Mayhem on Monday* was ... I was going to say *amazing* but that's so overused it's become trite and predictable, but I can't think of a better word. I was doing very little to change the prose in Trilby's pages and pages of notes. I rearranged many of them, and had to squint to read much of the spidery handwriting in the notes interspersed between the typed lines, but … yeah, they were just so good. I had to make the writing fuller, what he used to call *the lacy stuff*, but it was easy. Satisfying.

This was a Trilby from before my time with him. The man I'd worked for had been this good, but he'd been more practiced. This was from back when he'd written his own "lacy stuff." He'd known how to avoid the very real peril of his work becoming out-of-date, whereas this Trilby had not.

The sapphires were described in wonderfully intricate detail, a long description that could have become boring but did not. After I read it and typed it, I read it again, almost seeing the stones in the sunlight, feeling their warmth against my skin. I could envision their facets and the shapes created by them. There was a wedding ring among them, fashioned with small chips of lesser stones, that made chills run down my spine. It made me get up and check the locks and pour a hefty glass of wine even though I seldom drank it while I was working.

If the legend wasn't real, it should have been.

They hadn't been found yet, obviously—it was way too early in the story—but Finlay Iverson was on the case.

I loved watching the lake wake up. Summer people weren't actually there yet, but they were coming on Friday nights to open their cottages and fishing shacks in preparation for the months to come. They spent the weekend when they came, and the tables at the back of the mercantile would sometimes be full by the time the regulars got there.

April offered several warm, sunny days toward its end. One of them was the last Wednesday, and the coffee group took steel brushes, soft-bristled whisk brooms, and cans of paint along with go-cups, to refurbish the park benches that surrounded the lake at intervals. We got more than half of the benches done, stopping when we got to the mercantile. We had so much paint on us—both flakes we'd scraped off and splotches of new—that Colby covered the table and chairs before he let us sit down.

Jax texted, MORE VANDALISM. MPD WILL CALL YOU.

The police department from Muskegon called within minutes to let me know someone had defaced my parking spot at the apartment building. They'd gotten pictures and forensic evidence and my neighbor had offered to paint over the obscenities. Would that be okay with me?

The conversation was short, on the order of the "just the facts, ma'am" type from old television shows. When I hung up, it was hard to breathe. I clutched the table's edge, staring blindly down at the little plate of charcuterie board items that had looked so good only moments before.

Don't let me throw up.

"Maggie?" Cari spoke from the end of the long table we'd created by pushing two together. "You okay?"

"Yes." I took a sip … no, a gulp, of the iced tea I'd ordered. "No."

I told them then, starting with when Trilby introduced me to his brother, who magically appeared the next night in a class I was taking on spreadsheets—I was stumped by them … still am—and ending with the phone call I'd just had. By the time I was done, Colby had joined us at the table and, remarkably, so had Sam.

I had no idea what he was doing here in the middle of the week, but was glad to see him nevertheless. When he scooted a chair in beside me and took my hand under the table, I felt unquantifiable relief.

"This neighbor," said Colby. "Do you trust him?"

"Yes." I didn't have to think about that. Jax had already been in the other second-floor apartment when I moved in after I got out of the hospital. He was a literal trust fund baby whose parents owned the apartment complex, but other than living in our high-security, high-rent building, he didn't live like one. He was dedicated to music, to his students, and to a certain young nurse who worked at Mercy Health Muskegon.

"What about the other neighbors?"

"I don't really know them. We nod and smile if we see each other, but everyone's gone a lot. The Bashams are a retired couple who have a boat they spend every minute on they can. The Parkers, who are probably in their late thirties, live in the other one. They travel for their jobs and they used to park in the carports so that Jax's and my cars wouldn't fit and we'd have to park on the street." We'd joked that maybe they though their last name entitled them to our spaces.

They rubbed me the wrong way, although I was willing to concede the carport thing might have been an oversight or a case of misinformation. I didn't think so, though. Jax and I had left them a bottle of wine and a dozen cookies to welcome them to the building and they'd never responded.

Gloria and Rick Basham, on the other hand, had invited us over to share the bottle we left for them.

They gave us fudge at Christmas. I gave them Mayhem books and Jax distributed gift cards to the Black Dog.

As far as I knew, none of us exchanged gifts with the Parkers. They reported Jax once, saying his drums disturbed them even though his practice room in the basement was soundproofed and not even under their apartment. Jax said they'd taken to stomping up and down the stairs and the length of both hallways as a meant-to-annoy exercise program. He thought they wore combat boots with taps on the soles and heels.

"They sound like a lot of fun," said Sadie.

"So, the attempted break-in and the vandalism on your parking space—do you think they have to do with Greg Mathis?" Cari sounded troubled. "Do you believe you're being warned?"

I wanted to say no, of course not—it was all a coincidence—but I couldn't. When I tried to convince myself of that, the unrelenting knot in my stomach assured me I was wrong.

"It would be disingenuous to deny the possibility." Sam spoke from beside me.

"I know, and I don't. But he turned my life upside down once and I can never get that time back. It was my own fault that I was fooled by him, and I understand that completely, but what happened in the aftermath was his fault. He was the one who broke my hands and wrecked my piano and took away the person I was." My heartbeat did funny things and I felt breathless again. "I don't know what to do, but I have to do something."

"Let's make a plan," said Sam.

Rose got up from the table, going to the front of the store and coming back with a legal-size pad of light blue paper and a pen that advertised Squirrel Creek Foods. She handed them to Sam. "Here you go."

"How's your alarm here?" asked Colby, who had been a city policeman in Detroit before he and Rose bought the mercantile and moved to the lake.

"State of the art, and Uncle Bill just checked everything on it. But do you think Greg knows about the lake?" I addressed the question to Sam, knowing it was likely wishful thinking on my part. If others bought into it, maybe it would be true.

"I'd be surprised if he doesn't," said Sam, the words sounding forced. "I think he knows a lot more about his brother's life than anyone was aware of."

He'd written ALARM READY in thin, leggy letters. The pen tapped the pad as he waited for more.

"But I haven't changed anything," I protested. "Muskegon is still my legal address. I still go back there." I'd just been there with Uncle Bill and Aunt Lin. They'd had lunch with old friends and gone to the cemetery and I'd washed glasses for Scott at the Black Dog. When they picked me up there, Ellie and I were playing a slightly obscene board game with the baristas who worked the after-school shift.

We'd stopped by the apartment afterward. Jax had brought over the accumulation of mail he usually sent me in a Priority Mail envelope once a week. I was getting less sent to the apartment all the time and more to the Burl, but not on purpose. I didn't intend to change my legal address.

I didn't, but why not? Did I truly think that as long as my belongings were at the apartment and my mail was going into the cluster box and parcel locker in the building's tiny lobby, Greg would think I was still there full-time? Did I suppose that if he came to the apartment and I wasn't there, he'd just give up and go away … maybe far away where he'd have no effect on my life or on me ever again? Would he be content just to tape creepy things to the door and go on about his business?

Oh, sure. Who was I trying to kid?

"He'll keep looking until he finds me. He won't give up until I'm dead." *Or he is.*

"If it were me," said Haley Flynn, who hadn't said anything since I'd first spoken, "I'd vacate the apartment and disappear from Muskegon altogether." Her expression was … I don't know … stricken, maybe. Her eyes, as blue as her sons' were, looked almost muddy. "I'm not suggesting you change your name or anything like that, but don't give him a place to come back to, whether you're there or not."

As I watched, Amy reached for her mother-in-law's hand and squeezed it where it lay on the table. I looked from woman to woman around the table, at where Colby stood behind his wife with his hand on her shoulder. At Cari leaning over to whisper to Haley. At Sadie and Emily. I felt an ache I couldn't have described.

I would never be alone here. Whatever had happened to Haley, she hadn't borne it alone, and she was willing to open old wounds to help me make decisions.

My voice sounded raspy. "I know he'll find me even if he doesn't know yet that I'm here. I don't know how dangerous he is—" I stopped because my voice gave way altogether. Besides, what a lie that was. No one knew that better than I did.

"We don't have militia here," said Colby carefully. "We don't have the kind of weaponry you see in movies or on those off-the-wall news shows. Because of our location, though, we are prepared for"—he hesitated—"circumstances."

"Not all, by any means," said Emily, "but many of the full timers here are the walking wounded. That's why you never see some of the people who live here. It's not that they're snobs or naturally reclusive, it's that they've found personal safety in their aloneness. Having been in shoes much like yours, they've found their own way to make them fit." She hesitated. "Not all of them are model citizens. At least, they haven't always been."

My lifelong tendency to keep to myself has almost completely disappeared at the lake. For a moment, it struck me as odd that it would affect others in just the opposite way, but not odd at all that their wishes were respected.

It was time to leave Muskegon behind.

Chapter 14

I gave Jax whatever he wanted from the apartment furnishings and donated most of the rest of them. I shipped my mother's chest and its contents, my books, and other things that meant something to me to the lake, surprised I didn't have more than I did. How did one get to be my age with so little to show for it?

It was hard to think of Muskegon as my former home—I'd lived there my entire life. Never in a house, though. Never in a place that had more room than I needed. Tim and I used to laugh at the very idea of having extra space. Even if we'd been able to buy the house we wanted, it had been little more than a shotgun house. But we'd furnished it over and over in our minds and conversations.

I drove past it the day I turned over the keys to the apartment where I'd lived for the past five years. The little house on Sycamore Lane was charcoal gray now instead of the red it had been when it was our dream house. Two bicycles leaned against the east wall of the house, too small for adults, and I was happy to think a family lived there. I hoped they loved it.

The four of us from school had lunch together, making plans to meet for dinner more often, for them to weekend at the lake. I knew Ellie would always be there, but I wasn't sure about the others. Sometimes I don't give friendship enough credit for its strength, but I also understand that relationships come with different depths. I didn't talk to them about Greg's release from prison, which seems odd considering I'd told the Wednesday coffee group virtually everything.

Harper Loch was bursting with flowers. The boxes of books remained taped closed on the floor of the library, and the other cartons went from the moving company's panel truck to one of the garage bays and remained there. Eamon and Flynn carried my mother's chest into the Burl and set it under a pair of windows in the office. I created another set of steps from thick books and laid a quilt and her pillow on top of the chest for Chloe. She was in dog heaven.

I spent time planting even more flowers, adding to the layout Aunt Lin had designed while she was here. I had little experience with any sort of gardening, so I ended up moving half of what I put in place. At least I haven't killed any of it yet.

I paid the writers' group to come and spend an entire day. They did the heavy work, taught me some things about landscaping I didn't know—which was no trick, since I knew nothing—and signed on to come once a week and help keep the weeds from taking over. I fed them lunch and we had a mini-workshop on tenses before they worked a few more hours. It was an expensive day, but so worth it. The brush-up on tenses didn't hurt me any, either.

Jake and Emily were going to continue to do the mowing. I had planned to do it myself—I'd never driven a lawn tractor or even used a push mower—but watching them do it one time convinced me otherwise. Left on my own, I'd have gone tumbling down that hill more than once, and I couldn't envision it ending well.

Sam came late Friday morning for the weekend. He spent a lot of time walking through the flower beds with Chloe as his guide, and I wondered what was on his mind. I joined him when I'd gotten my words written for the day, taking coffee for him and a treat for Chloe. She barely noticed me when he was around. If Uncle Bill had been here, heaven knows how she would have divided her sketchy loyalties between those two loves of her life. I think they made her miss Trilby less.

We sat at the wrought iron bistro table I'd dragged out of the garage and spray-painted sage green. A citronella candle sat in a lacy metal holder in the middle of the table.

"How's the book coming?" Sam's cup touched mine in an unspoken toast to the day.

"It's amazing." It was getting way too easy for me to use that word in connection to Trilby's final book. I needed to branch out my vocabulary a bit. "It's harder to put together because he wrote different parts at different times, so even though the notes are linear, they don't sound alike. So, I'll be writing along and have to go back and put it all in the same voice. It's all very Trilby, but he must have started it when he was in his forties." I hesitated before going on. "It's about the sapphires. The family legend."

He set down his cup, "Really?"

I nodded. "I think they truly do exist. Or did. You wouldn't believe the description he wrote. I felt as if they were right in my hands. And they were warm. I know the warmth isn't real, but sapphires can be heated or unheated, which has to do with whether they're processed by man or not. The unheated ones are more valuable, but reading about the differences gave me the illusion of warmth. I'm not sure it was Trilby's intent, and I'll be anxious to find out if it affects readers the same way."

"Were the ones in the legend heated or unheated?"

"Both—at least, in the book they were—so their worth varied a lot." I laughed. "I've never felt the urge to jump ahead when I've worked on the books. Trilby processed the stories aloud so even though the Mayhem books are mysteries, I always knew what was going on—except that there was always a surprise, an *aha!* part of the mystery he tested out on me to see if I caught it. But he'd never talked about this story, at least to me. He never mentioned the sapphires. The whole book is an *aha.* And I still have no answers."

"But you think the sapphires are real?"

I nodded, feeling foolish even as I did. "Think of it, Sam. I worked for Trilby for two-thirds of my life. I knew the Lunchroom and Mayhem stories as well as he did—better, sometimes. But I never had the first clue about this. The closest he ever came to mentioning sapphires was when he frowned at the wedding ring Greg gave me." I stopped, thinking of— "That ring's in the book, and he wrote that part long ago. Before I ever met Greg or even knew he existed."

The thought of the ring made me shudder. The police still had it, and I didn't know what to do with it when they gave it back to me. I gestured at our surroundings, needing to change the subject. "Do you like the flowers?"

He nodded. "Mom would have loved them." He smiled at me, the expression holding me as still as if he were touching me. "She'd have loved you."

I wondered at life's algorithms. We'd known each other all our adult lives, including lots of single years when we were both dating other people. We'd cried in our beer together more than once, but never looked across the table while we were doing it. At least, not consciously. I wondered sometimes how long the yearning for more had been there.

We talked about plans for the weekend, about the growth in church attendance that delighted Cari, and about the likelihood I'd never get enough of the stuff out of the garage for me to park in it. He asked about the shed that hovered at the edge of the woods. It was more of a small barn, complete with crossbucks on its front door and a painted quilt block on the outside peak of the gabled roof.

I wondered if there was more to Sam's visit than just coming to the lake for a few days. He didn't seem edgy, as he sometimes did, but something was on his mind. I hadn't eaten breakfast, so I was ready for lunch. I was all set to say so when he spoke.

"He's been seen in Muskegon."

The words pinged against the tabletop; at least, that's the way they sounded when I heard them. I thought if Sam hadn't been there, sitting across from me with his gaze holding mine, I might have folded in on myself.

I never wanted to be that dependent on anyone, but for the first time, I wondered if the real reason Trilby had left me the Burl was to give me a safe place for when Greg reappeared. Had he thought I couldn't take care of myself?

For that matter, *could* I take care of myself?

"Don't." Sam's voice was firm.

"Don't what?"

"Don't sit there thinking you have to handle this all on your own because that's what big girls do."

"How do you know that's what I'm doing?"

"Because I know you. Your neighbors here aren't kidding, though, Maggie. They're going to be here for you. They're like Jax times eighty-five."

His tone of voice more than the words he said stopped the train of thought I was riding to destruction. He did know me, and I knew him, in ways I don't think either of us had ever realized. We'd never verbalized it because we hadn't needed to. Or didn't think we'd needed to.

"I'm afraid someone will be hurt," I said. "How would I live with it if someone I cared about got hurt because I made a stupid, stupid mistake when I met Greg Mathis?"

"Trilby introduced him to you, didn't he?"

I nodded. "He had to. Greg came to the office one day, unannounced. Then he showed up in a class I was taking at the community college."

"Did you blame him?"

"Who, Trilby? Of course not. He didn't know what his brother was capable of. He didn't trust him, but he never really explained why. He'd been an adult when Greg was adopted—they'd never lived in the same house. It's different for me—I *do* know. I know what he's capable of and that he doesn't care who he hurts."

He got up, stretching, and reached for my hand. "Want to walk around the lake? I need to look in on

Cari." His smile crooked up in the way I liked so much. "Favorite uncle status has so much heavy responsibility attached to it."

"Oh, I'm sure it does." I put my phone in my pocket. "Let me get Chloe."

"That dog's more trouble than she's worth."

"How's Wilbur?" I asked sweetly. "You should bring him along sometime. Just give him his meds before you put him in the car."

Sam's big cat was lovely; he was also a nervous traveler who either howled or threw up every time he had to go to the vet.

"I may just do that. Usually, I have to have a cat-sitter when I'm gone for longer than overnight, but maybe you could keep him instead. I don't know if he and Chloe would get along, but this place is plenty big enough for Wilbur to have his own suite of rooms."

I laughed, although I wouldn't mind being Wilbur's foster mom. Like Sam, I wasn't sure how Chloe would feel about it, but it would be fun to try it. Besides, it would mean seeing more of Sam.

I couldn't believe how much I liked that thought.

We got quiet as we walked. He didn't take my hand as he sometimes did, and I wished he would. I felt ridiculously vulnerable. Especially after he led the way off Enoch Trace and up one of the graveled driveways to the path that went around the second row. I never came up here, although I knew some of the residents. A few of the ones who lived here year-round attended church; most of them stayed to themselves. Since Emily had mentioned them, I'd started worrying about them.

Although most of the cottages were well kept, a few of them were not. I wished they looked nicer, but I appreciated the respect for privacy observed by the people on the lake. The mobile homes were all old—I doubted if any of them were more than ten feet wide and forty or fifty feet long, but age had little to do with appearance. Several of them were completely cute. I couldn't believe I used that descriptor; Finlay Iverson would be aghast. However, it was accurate. They were painted in the same colors as other cottages, with decks or screened porches built on and flowerbeds and window boxes that were teeming with bright blooms.

"They're talking about widening this path and opening it to cars," I said, stopping so that Chloe could visit the wildflowers that grew along the way. "I heard at the mercantile that a few more lots have been cleared and sold, and people want an actual road they can drive something bigger than a golf cart on."

"I can understand that."

"I can, too." But I hated to see Harper Loch change. I knew access was a problem in more than one area around the lake. While we had hardly any traffic, the vehicles we did have needed to be able to move.

The realization that I was thinking in terms of *we* probably pleased me more than it should have. Ten minutes later, when Cari greeted her uncle with a squeal and a hug that should have cut off his air supply, I wondered what it would be like to be someone's aunt, which took the *we* consideration down a road I hadn't dared consider.

"He called at the office and said he just wanted to give us his condolences for our loss." Tom Winterroad's voice was terse. "I thanked him and hung up. Dan had a call from him the same day. Mathis didn't ask for any information and we didn't give him any, but I wanted you to know."

It was Thursday. It had been six days since Sam told me Greg had been seen in Muskegon. He was on parole, but free. There was nothing overtly wrong about him calling Trilby's sons.

"Thank you," I said. "I'm sorry to have—"

"You have nothing to be sorry for," Tom interrupted. "Just stay safe, Maggie. You're our sister of the heart, after all. And I didn't make that up—Miriam said it and she's right."

After talking to him, I carried my laptop outside, determined not to be frightened into hiding behind closed doors. Chloe followed me. She loved being outside since the weather had warmed into the seventies most days.

For my own sake, I wanted to believe Greg had been rehabilitated by his time in prison, but I knew better. As if in response to the thought, my fingers ached. It was a little skewed, I admitted to myself, that I was able to put the rape behind me...at least, sort of. But he committed the rape and the hitting had been because he wanted to rape and hit someone—it wouldn't have mattered who it was. I was able to separate myself from it. But breaking my fingers when he knew typing and playing piano were the things that defined me more than anything else? No amount of talking to a therapist had ever eased that particular anger; the damage to my hands had been so personal I hadn't found a distancing compartment to put it into.

Sam had hung a motion detector with a bell on the back of the house when he was here so that I would be more likely to hear people approach, since nearly everyone at the lake got around on bicycles, golf carts, or their feet. I'd protested, but not very much. I knew anyone scaling the Burl's ramparts after dark would manage to do so without making noise, but I still liked being forewarned when I was outside.

It rang as I worked that afternoon. Chloe, awakened from her nap in the sunshine, yapped irritably, then tucked her nose back into her tail and went back to sleep. What a watchdog.

As I got up, Ellie called out a hello and came to where I sat, slinging a backpack to one side and pulling me into a hug. “I’m off work for the rest of the week and I have come to stay until Sunday night. I didn’t call because I had a feeling you’d tell me not to bother because you’re busy and you’re grumpy. Am I right? Is there coffee?”

Ellie is much more…enthusiastic than I am. I have been a loyal follower of her leadership for forty-some years, since I sat in front of her in second grade and she copied my single-digit arithmetic problems until she figured out I didn’t have them right, either. I know when she’s faking.

I turned to head into the house, picking up her backpack. “It’s Thursday. You never take off just for the heck of it. You heard from him.”

She was right behind me. “I saw him.”

I almost stumbled, and her arm came through mine. We stood there for an instant on the middle step that led onto the big back porch. One of us was quaking, and the other one was holding my arm far too tightly “You know,” I said, my voice quiet, “I’ve always found strength in being a loner. But I’m finding out my real strength comes from my friends, both old and new. How can I have just figured that out?”

We stepped inside and I looked around my beloved kitchen, at the shards of colored light being painted on its walls by the sunlight coming through the transom window. “Maybe that’s the lesson taught by this place.”

"Maybe." Ellie freed her arm from mine and went to the coffee bar.

"Want a late lunch?"

"You bet."

As much as I love to cook, one of my favorite comfort meals is bologna sandwiches with lettuce, cheese, and mayo. With potato chips—lots of them—on the side straight from the bag without benefit of a plate. We worked together silently, seamlessly, a product of long friendship. I'd helped her study so much when she was in nursing school and later, when she took more classes to become a nurse practitioner, that I thought she should invite me to join her in her practice. However, when she started talking about body fluids, I gave up on that idea.

We ate in the alcove, making plans for the next few days, most of which involved food. We talked about Sam and Scott, a conversation that went south quickly. It would have been ridiculous when we were sixteen—it was much more so now. When Ellie used the words *all the way* in her very best ninth-grade voice, I knew it was time to stop.

"I need to get more writing done," I said.

"Outside? Go ahead. I'll get my tablet and transcribe some notes from yesterday." She unzipped her backpack.

I was standing at the table outside staring at the screen of my laptop when Ellie came outside. "Maggie?"

She may have said it more than once before I looked up. "Where did you see him?"

"He came to the office this morning. He was there when I got to work. I had a few patients to see before I came here. The receptionist had already unlocked the front door and he stepped inside as soon as she did. He asked if it was all right if he waited until I got there and she didn't have any reason to tell him no."

I shivered. And I couldn't stop.

"He said he was so sorry for the harm he'd caused. He wanted me to tell you that. I told him I would." Her hand was on my forearm, holding firmly. "Then I told him to leave and not ever come back."

"He didn't ask where I was?"

She shook her head. "Presumably he wouldn't have expected me to tell him." Her hand tightened. "Maggie?" she said again.

I pointed at the screen, where my words had been deleted and new ones added after we went in the house.

NICE PLACE MAGGIE. WHAT DID YOU DO FOR OLD TRILBY TO EARN THIS. LOOKS LIKE I HAD YOUR NUMBER ALL ALONG. SEEMS TO ME YOU OWE ME AT LEAST HALF OF ALL THIS. YOU NEVER SHOULD OF GOT ME PUT IN PRISON.

"Let's go into the house," said Ellie.

I took my phone out of my pocket and called first the sheriff's office and then Colby. "I don't know what to do," I told him. "I don't want to leave my laptop out here in case he's still around, but I don't want to touch it, either."

"I'll be there in a few minutes. Don't hang up."

Ellie was staring over at the motion detector on the corner of the house. "It didn't ring. How did he get past the bell?" The color washed from her face so completely I was afraid she was going to faint. "Oh, dear God, Maggie, he must have followed me here."

Chapter 15

I shook my head and grasped Ellie's shoulders. They trembled under my hands. "He couldn't have known you were coming here. You were at work. As far as he knew, you were staying there." I didn't want to tell her it had been my first thought, too. He was finding people so fast, talking to them, apologizing to them—what was to say he didn't have some kind of creepy watch on Ellie's activities? He'd known—and resented—how close we are.

In a disconnected moment, I thought maybe he wanted to apologize to me, too. To promise to never approach me or anyone I knew again. He used to say he had friends in Canada—maybe he would expatriate himself there and never come back.

That hope didn't last long, though.

It had been only a matter of time before he found me, although I had to admit I hoped it might be *more* time.

I let her go and stood close enough to her that we propped each other up, just as we always had. "It's not like my being here was a real secret. Even if I didn't tell that many people where I was moving to, it wouldn't have been that hard to figure out. I'm sure if you googled it, the contents of Trilby's will are out there somewhere." I'd minded enough people's private business in the name of research for the Mayhem books to know it wasn't always that difficult. There'd been times I'd felt like a walking, talking tabloid.

"We're doing no harm," Trilby assured me when I muttered about feeling creepy.

Colby was there, as he'd promised, in a few minutes. Ben, the sheriff's deputy, took only a little longer.

He stared at the screen. "That note to you is all that's on here. Was it an open file?"

I wasn't surprised Greg had deleted my manuscript. Just as he had my friendship with Ellie, he'd resented my writing and my partnership with Trilby. He'd never had a relationship with his brother, so it seemed unfair that I had. He'd tried to make it into something salacious, to insinuate that Trilby had been more than my boss and my friend. He'd threatened to tell Claire "everything," and I'd told him to go ahead, but I'd hated him for it. I still hated him for it. I'd loved Trilby, but no more than I'd loved Claire.

The last fight with Greg, the most violent one, had been over the half-penny-a-word bonus Trilby paid me every day I worked, keeping track in a notebook from the words CHAPTER 1 FINLAY IVERSON ANSWERED HIS PHONE that started every book to WELL, THANK GOODNESS THAT'S OVER, the ones that ended it. It had indeed built up to a tidy sum thanks to the financial advisor Trilby and I shared. and it went into an account Greg couldn't access no matter how hard he tried.

"It was open," I said. "It was backed up, except what I wrote this morning. I'm not sure that can be recaptured." I wasn't technologically savvy enough to find things when I lost them in the depths of my computer's hard drive, but I knew people who were. It didn't matter that much, though—a few hundred words were a small loss, especially since I still had the notes they were taken from. Although the printed sheets I'd been working with were gone from the table, I still had the original notes on paper as well as on the thumb drive that had been in the pocket of the blue binder. Greg would be disappointed not to have caused more damage.

He'd try harder next time.

What a strange afternoon and evening it was. I wasn't surprised when Sam arrived, although I hadn't called him. Ellie looked guilty enough that I knew who had. Cari came. Rose brought a meat and cheese tray from the mercantile's deli. When Colby asked who was minding the store, she said Jim the dog was and got a laugh from everyone except her husband. "Eamon's there. With Jim's help, he probably runs it better than either of us does."

"Well, that's true." Colby nodded agreement. "He's eighteen and doesn't know the meaning of tired yet."

Rose waved a dismissive hand when I tried to pay her. "This is rural Michigan, remember? Any excuse for a potluck."

Except for when I was home, with the doors locked and the alarm on, it appeared I would spend little time by myself. I was nonplused by the planning my neighbors were doing. It felt a little like the gathering of a militia.

"Not militia." Jake shook his head when I said as much. "It's like we've already talked about—we just have to have a certain level of preparedness when we live this far out."

I knew that, and understood it, but I was still dismayed that I'd brought danger to this place I loved. What if someone got hurt? Besides me, I mean. How would I deal with that? How would this close-knit band of neighbors deal with it? Would they want me to leave and take my scarred past with me?

"The late-day walkers will swing by and get you," said Cari, "and we'll have Wednesday coffee at your house for a while if you don't mind. I don't believe the assailant is long on courage. He's not about to attack a bunch of women. Especially ones like us."

"You got that right," said Sam, and laughter fell soft and helpful into the conversation.

"Would he steal, do you think?" asked Haley, who'd come by after she got off work in Placer. "If so, we could put a leaky boat by your dock. There are a lot of them around."

We laughed again, louder this time—we'd all seen the episode of *The Andy Griffith Show* that involved a leaky boat and some bad guys.

It was surreal.

Darkness had fallen by the time everyone was gone except Ellie. Even Sam went to sleep in the fishing shack to "break it in for summer," which meant he'd hired a couple of the writers' group boys to clean it up and he wanted to check on it.

"I'm surprised he left," said Ellie, when we were sitting in the living room in our pajamas with wine and the leftovers from the tray Rose had brought. "I'd have thought he was protective."

"He is." I'd been surprised at first, too, but protective or not, he wasn't the smothering sort. He'd known I couldn't have stood that. "I think he gets that at the end of the day, regardless of the plans made, I want to be the one to worry about my own pretty little head. Well, Uncle Bill and me—I can only get so much independence past him."

We talked far into the night, with me catching up on her kids and how things were going with Scott and her wanting to know more about the Maggie-and-Sam romance. If that was indeed what it was.

It was, and we picked up the conversation where I'd cut if off earlier that day. We were both old enough and private enough that we kept our sex lives to ourselves. And, it seems, each other. We'd replaced discussion of birth control options with much bemoaning of the effects of menopause, but we laughed just as hard as we always had.

Then we talked about Trilby's last story, and her insights had me running for a notepad and pen. "I feel like Trilby," she said when I came back.

I wrote down what she'd suggested, thinking of my relationship with Trilby. Although Ellie was one of the few who knew everything about it, she'd never really understood it—not completely, anyway.

She'd thought my name should have been on the front of the books where I'd done either most of or all the writing. He'd suggested it, too, and had come close to insisting we use *only* my name on the Lunchroom Mysteries, because I'd written every word of them. I'd named the young detectives and created their families and given them their hair and eye colors.

But the ideas had all been Trilby's, even after he was no longer able to do the composition. The outlines of the Mayhem books had all been painstakingly complete. While he'd had little to do with the children's books, their conception had been his. He'd talked me through the middle chapters when I'd written myself into corners.

To be crass about it, the money had been in his name, not mine. While people knew I was a more involved assistant than most, hardly anyone knew how much I actually wrote. I was sorry Greg had become aware of it. He'd liked my income too well to interfere with how I earned it, but he'd held the knowledge over my head. He hadn't minded hurting me; he would have hurt his brother just as easily.

He didn't, did he, Trilby? It was as we thought on that last day, wasn't it?

"Did he have dementia?" asked Ellie. "Was that why you did the writing in the later years?"

I'd wondered about that occasionally. His memory had begun to fail after Claire died, but neither he nor his sons had mentioned it, so I didn't either. "I don't think he did, but he was never able to write after Claire's first bout with cancer. At least not much, although he could still lay out the story just as he always had. At the end of the day, it was a business. We became partners and we made it work." I shrugged. "I didn't want to be well known, and he thrived on it."

I checked the alarm before going to bed, took the gun from its safe place and put it in the drawer of the bedside stand, and stood for a long time looking out the bedroom windows at the lake across Enoch Trace. The water lay still, although I fancied I saw shadows everywhere I looked. Was that someone sitting on the park bench close to the Burl's dock? Were there lights in the little graveyard beside the church?

I closed the vertical blinds and got into bed with Chloe snuggled in beside me. While I am religious, I never feel as if I'm deeply so. However, on this night in the Burl, I felt the lightening presence of the prayers of friends. And I was grateful.

What a surprise that I slept not only immediately, but without interruption. I wouldn't have woken when I did if it hadn't been for Choe's insistence. I let her out, then got myself a cup of coffee from the Keurig before joining her, taking a towel with me to wipe nighttime's moisture from the bistro table and chairs that had become my favorite place to greet the day.

Chloe ran across the yard, her ears flapping, barking nonstop. Didn't dogs need to breathe when they were running *and* yapping? When she got close to where I was, she stopped, stared at me for a few seconds, then turned and ran back toward the shed.

"Oh, for Pete's sake." Irritated, the towel still in my hand, I followed her, hoping it wasn't a snake she wanted me to see. I wasn't as scared of them as Ellie was, but that didn't mean I wanted to be friends with them.

The morning was bright, with the early sun making diamonds in the dewy grass and soaking my canvas slip-ons. Chloe stopped again, and I almost tripped over her. “Chloe, what is your problem?”

Then I saw the kitten. Surely too tiny to be separated from its mother, it was also terribly hurt, the skin on its side sliced open and a long, narrow cut on its belly. Its tail was a bloody little stump. It couldn’t possibly be alive. Nothing that small could lose that much blood and still live. Chloe was looking at me again. *Do something.*

“Okay, okay,” I muttered, kneeling. The kitten, which resembled a mangled grayish-white rat as much as a cat, lay on the grass. A small shoebox was there, too, lying on its side and wet with dew and congealed blood.

I gathered the broken little body into the damp towel and stood, nearly dropping the bundle when it stirred in my hand. By the time I got to the house, with Chloe following anxiously at my heels, the bundle was squeaking.

Ellie was in the kitchen, her auburn hair piled on top of her head. She smiled when I came in, lifting a coffee cup in greeting, then frowned at the towel I carried. “What have you got?”

If you don’t have a vet on the premises, a nurse practitioner is the next best thing, especially one who’s raised two kids, complete with accompanying injuries and the bringing home of stray animals. “Oh,” she said when I opened the towel. "Oh, poor baby. There's a vet's office in Placer, Mags. Call them."

I thumbed over my phone, finding the clinic's number. They weren't open yet, but Dr. Lisa was on her way to work. She would stop by the Burl. Yes, she knew where it was. Ten minutes tops.

There truly are things I love about living in what is euphemistically referred to as the back of the beyond. More of them every day.

"Who would do this kind of thing?" Ellie muttered.

Who indeed?

While the phone was still in my hand, I called the sheriff's office. Ben, the deputy who'd grown up in a cottage across the lake and gone to school with Flynn Squires, said he'd be there soon. "Don't touch the box," he said.

I had no intention of touching it. I had no intention of even leaving the house—maybe ever again. I didn't know where Greg was, but I was sure he was close.

What do you want? What more can you do to me?

He could do a lot. I knew that. I hadn't written about crimes for nothing. As wonderful as the support from the people at the lake and the sheriff's office was, there was no Finlay Iverson here, nor did I know how to write the ending of this story.

The veterinarian arrived within minutes, and she and Ellie combined forces to medicate the kitten and stitch its gaping wounds. “Euthanasia is warranted,” Lisa Sanders said gently, “simply by the breadth of his injuries, or we will do what we can. It’s up to you.”

She called the kitten *he*, not *it.* “He deserves a chance. Please do whatever you can.”

By the time Sam arrived, we were all gathered around the table, including the deputy. He was drinking coffee as he took down information and occasionally stroked the little cat’s head between his ears. Ben, Dr. Lisa, and Ellie discussed the best way to avoid euthanizing Ezekiel. *Everything deserves a name.* I wasn’t sure where I’d read it, but I believed it, and Chloe and I settled on Ezekiel. I rubbed his head gently, too. It was the only part of him that didn’t seem to be damaged—both a surprise and a blessing. I looked up when Sam stood in the doorway.

“Coffee?” I asked, getting up, and he waved me to my seat.

“I’ll get it.”

His hand rested for a moment on my shoulder as he passed. “What happened to the cat? He looks like the lawnmower got him.”

“Meet Ezekiel. I think he’s the latest victim in the Greg Mathis horror show.”

“Good God,” said Ellie from her spot as veterinary assistant. “What is it?”

“It’s one for the books.” There was wonder in Lisa’s voice. “I thought it was going to be a grub.”

I’d seen grubs being removed on TV shows featuring veterinarian clinics. I was weirdly fascinated by the procedure. “Let me see.”

The infiltrating object wasn’t a grub, although the hole left by the small blue stone Lisa’s tweezers released looked like the ones on Dr. Pol’s TV show.

“Someone knew what they were doing,” Dr. Lisa told the deputy, dropping the untouched stone—or piece of glass; I couldn’t tell which it was—into the little evidence bag he held forth. “As ugly as these wounds are, they avoided his head. This stone was inserted under the skin but no deeper. The cuts on his side and his belly are huge, but no bones were broken, no organs penetrated. His tail was partially amputated—a caudectomy—and it was rather neatly done. A vet I worked for said people used to do it all the time just because they thought it made kittens cuter. This one’s at least part Siamese, though. I can’t imagine anyone doing it for that reason with him. Although some people will if the tail’s crooked or notched, most don’t.”

... a vet I worked for ... Trilby and Greg’s father had been a vet and both boys had helped him at different times. Greg would know how to keep from doing mortal injury to a kitten, but he wouldn’t care one way or the other if he did. Although no one would have

looked at the lump under the skin where the gemstone had been if the kitten had died.

We'd never had pets, but Chloe hadn't liked Greg. I'd never given that much thought, because until she met her favorite lake residents, she hadn't liked many people at all. She sulked in the office closet when anyone came to see Trilby. He always left the door ajar for her, but she wouldn't come out until the person who encroached in her territory left.

I told the deputy that, and he wrote it down. At least, the part about Greg. He probably didn't care about Chloe and the closet door.

"How was the fish shack?" I asked Sam when he slid into the chair beside mine after refilling everyone's cups.

"Very neat." He frowned. "It's not natural that kids are so good at cleaning stuff up. I just expected the floor to be swept and spiders to be cleared out of the sink. Instead, the windows had been washed and everything. It even smelled more like pine cleaner than fish."

I gasped. "The horror of it!"

"Yeah, Harp and Trilby wouldn't be happy. They always said Mom and Claire were way too clean. There were a few Founders beer cans on the path to the lake. Renewed my faith in adolescence."

"They don't drink." It had been part of a long discussion over tacos one night. "Not that they haven't, but they don't."

"What makes you so sure?"

I grinned at him. "They were caught. It ruined their social lives for a while. Kids who live in the country don't want to lose their driving privileges."

"Makes sense."

Something clicked. "What kind did you say?"

"Founders."

"Lager, by any chance?" I asked, dread making my voice sound odd to my own ears.

"Yeah, as a matter of fact." Something in my voice must have caught his attention. "Don't tell me—it was Finlay Iverson's brew of choice. That would be too weird."

"No," I said. "Finlay drinks Guinness. Greg Mathis's choice was Founders Premium Lager."

Ben looked up from the notes he was taking on a tablet.

It shouldn't have meant anything. Lots of people drank lager, and many of them preferred Founders—it was a Michigan beer, after all. The Parkers, my neighbors in Muskegon, drank copious amounts of it and weren't careful with their cans and bottles, which had irritated the rest of us. Greg would have tossed the cans onto the path instead of finding a recycling receptacle to put them in, too. "That's what people in jail are for," he used to jeer when I objected to him littering. "Inmates need something to do."

How ironic. How horribly ironic.

"The cans are in the recycle bin," said Sam. "DNA. I feel like an idiot because I didn't think of it at the time. I can show you, Ben, if it will be any help."

Sam, Chloe, and I went for a walk around the lake later that day. Ben had collected the cans from where Sam put them in the recycle bin and told me three times I wasn't a bother. Ellie was having a late lunch with Sadie in Placer. As big as the Burl was, I felt confined there.

I knew Sam was disturbed because the empty cans at the fish shack hadn't clicked with him as being of possible importance. "I'd be a failure as Finlay, wouldn't I?"

I couldn't see him failing at anything, although I doubted he'd been all that good at marriage. Some people just weren't. I thought his wife was one who had likely needed patience from her partner—maybe more of it than Sam had to give.

"You don't need to be Finlay." I looked up at him, shaking my head. "You just need to be Sam. You're the best Sam there is."

Was I, right in the middle of my personal maelstrom of panic and dread and regret, *flirting* with Sam Eldridge? He was my friend. My lawyer. My ukulele partner—although we were admittedly better together when we confined our musical performances to instruments we could actually play. The fact that I thought he was the handsomest man I'd ever met was just a late-in-friendship observation, as was the warm ripple of my long-inactive girl parts that accompanied his presence. I'm fifty-two years old, for heaven's sake. I don't have a flat stomach or perky boobs. My libido was …

Well, alive and well is what it was. Even with every nerve I had jangling with worry over what would happen next. Would the next kitten be dead? Would I? I thought there might be something wrong with sexual thoughts cavorting around in my head and other areas, too, but I couldn't for the life of me think of what it could be.

We'd been playing around since I'd come to the lake, building on the feelings we were discovering—at least, I thought he was discovering them, too. But I wasn't in a place to act on them; if Greg Mathis's release from prison took me down a rabbit hole of horror, I couldn't take anyone else with me.

Maybe we could ... No maybe to it, I told myself forcefully. While I'd never been a fan of purely physical relationships, they did have their place. Right now, that was all Sam and I could have.

He held my gaze long enough for me to realize I was lying to myself. He took my hand. "I don't know where we are," he said, his voice so low I had to strain to hear, "or where we're going, but even if all we have going is friendship, Maggie North, we're in this together. Okay?"

"Be still, my soul, be still …" The line was from an A. E. Housman poem I'd read when Tim was alive and I thought life was full of promise. I'd memorized its first stanza and held onto the words through those days of so much love and so much loss I knew I'd never see its like again.

I hadn't, either. But Sam's eyes, the shade of which I'd determined from a color wheel were cerulean, made me think I should add a *yet* to that thought. Because *together* sounded more wonderful than I could have ever imagined.

Especially now.

Chapter 16

Ellie wanted to drag me back to Muskegon with her. "If I call Aunt Lin, she'll make you come," she threatened, standing beside her open car door early Sunday evening.

"If you call Aunt Lin, I'll never, ever forgive you and I'll take your kids out of my will no matter how much I love them." Ellie's son and daughter were grown—they had little ones of their own now—but I didn't love them any less.

She snorted. "You'll just slip the money to them when my back's turned the way you always have." She leaned in, hugging me hard, and I clung for a minute or so. "Be safe," she whispered. "Just be safe. I love you.'

"Love you back." I drew back after wiping my eyes on the shoulder of the PLACER HIGH SCHOOL T-shirt the writer kids had given her when they made her an honorable member of their group after she gave them valuable advice on a technical writing exercise.

They hadn't given me a shirt, and she'd been sure to remind me often that *honorable* was ever so much better than *honorary*.

The house was quiet when I went inside. Even Sam was fishing. Chloe went to her favorite spot at the French doors in the dining alcove where she could keep an eye on both woods activity and the kitten lying on a heating pad in a willow basket from the garage, and I poured myself a generous glass of wine and went into the office. Ezekiel slept most of the time, but Chloe stayed by her side, occasionally lapping her tongue over the kitten's head.

I didn't think I'd been alone for a minute since Ellie had arrived. As much as I loved her and liked Sam—I wasn't going there with the *love* word—and as much as I liked my neighbors and appreciated the proverbial circling of the wagons, I needed some time to be … just Maggie North. Although I'd become much more social since coming to the lake—*much* more social—I still needed the breathing space afforded by alone time.

I hadn't written since the morning Greg infiltrated the backyard of the Burl. As gripping as Trilby's last story was, it had slipped to the back of my mind in the past days. It didn't take long, though, to draw me back in. I reconstructed what had been lost and wrote steadily until darkness fell, answering Cari's text with THE MUSE HAS LANDED when I skipped the evening walk. The wine sat untouched as Finlay Iverson threaded his way through the labyrinth of conflict and chaos of a relationship story that already had more twists and turns in it than the Harper Loch Road.

Finlay had been in love. Really. It seemed a bit late to bring that to light. But, as always with Trilby and Finlay, it was working.

Chloe appeared at the doorway into the office, and I realized she wasn't the only one who was hungry. A text came in from Sam as I headed to the kitchen. AT THE MERCANTILE. WANT TO SHARE A PIZZA?

I smiled, feeling the anticipatory leap under my ribs that wasn't that much of a surprise anymore. SURE.

The answer came back in seconds. FIFTEEN MINUTES.

The bell on the corner of the house chimed twenty minutes later, and Chloe and I went out through the mudroom.

"Dang it," said Sam, when I opened the door. "What if that hadn't been me?"

I rolled my eyes at him as he passed me on the way in. "Just because you were late? Do you want to cat outside or in?"

"In. There's a nip in the air."

"Good heavens, you'd think it was Michigan, wouldn't you?" I set plates on the quilted placemats on the counter. "Beer? Are you driving back to Muskegon tonight?"

“Yes and no. I’m going to give summer hours a shot, just being in the office Tuesday through Thursday unless I have to be in court.”

I frowned at him. “Are you doing that because of me?”

“No, absolutely not.” He stopped moving, pinning me with a solemn gaze. “Even if you paid me for everything I do, pizza delivery tips only cover so much.”

“But I’m a *good* tipper.”

Flirting again. I liked it. I liked how it made me feel, the look he got in his eyes. I wondered if mine had the same expression. What was the word I’d thought earlier? Oh, yeah … anticipatory.

So much of what had happened in my life this year had been—whether I liked the thought of it or not—engineered by Trilby. Had he planted seeds in my relationship with Sam, too? There was no denying he was the reason we’d met in the first place, the reason we had frequent enough contact to develop a friendship that had spanned several decades.

“I can do a lot from here.” Sam put pizza on both plates and set them on the placemats. “The paralegals in the office can do courthouse runs on Monday and Friday if necessary.”

I followed with beer and another glass of wine—one I intended to drink.

"How are you doing?" Sam asked, when we were seated across from each other. "Are you worried?"

I frowned, sipped from my soft red, then sipped again. "More fatalistic, I think, although I hope not literally. I have no doubt he'll come back and he'll intimidate me again, but I can't hide in my room with my gun in my hand and wait." Not the whole truth, but most of it.

"You can't. I agree with that, but you do need to be careful."

"I am." It had taken me years to stop looking over my shoulder at every unexpected noise, and now I was almost back at square one. Except that this time, I expected Greg Mathis. There was an old saying about the devil you know being better than the one you didn't, and I was counting on that and being cautious accordingly. Cautious. Not scared.

In a pig's eye.

"But you hate it, don't you? It's making you relive things you don't want to."

"It is." When I'd played the piano last, I'd looked down at my damaged hands and stopped suddenly, unable to finish "Morning Has Broken," a song I loved and knew as well as "Für Elise," the first piece I'd ever learned to play without benefit of sheet music. "I'm back to locking everything, checking the locks, then checking them again. When the phone rings, I look to see who's calling before I answer, which I never do. I'm leery of sitting outside, of walking by myself, of staying alone even though I've lived alone much of my adult life."

I could hear my voice rising, feel the acceleration of my heartbeat and the heat and pressure of tears behind my eyes. "It makes me so damn mad, Sam. *So* mad. And I don't know what to do. I can't depend on the whole lake community to protect me every minute until the shoe finally drops." I stopped, shaking all over, then said again, "I don't know what to do."

It was all a pretense, the calm, the whole *que sera, sera* thing.

I was scared. I was scared to death.

Thinking of my hands, remembering I'd had to stop playing "Morning Has Broken," had torn down the emotional wall I'd built so carefully.

From the fallen rocks of that wall came every word I'd held back from the minute I'd had to confront the fact that I'd married an abuser. Between bites of the mercantile's most excellent pizza, I talked and talked and talked.

I had been brave for Aunt Lin and Uncle Bill because I didn't want them to worry about me. I'd been brave for Ellie because I didn't want her to feel responsible for me. I'd been brave with the lake "militia" because they had no reason to risk anything for the purpose of having my back.

But I wasn't brave. I wasn't brave at all. I was a middle-aged woman who'd been hurt and was afraid of being hurt again and I didn't know where to go from here. For the third time, with my fingers clenched into fists so tight my nails bit into my palms, I said it again in a voice aching and strained, "I don't know what to do."

Sam and I always hugged when we saw each other now, and we'd shared embraces that fell deliciously outside the parameters of friendship, but when he stepped around the end of the counter and took me into his arms, it was pure comfort.

I don't know how long we stood like that. Chloe came and wound between our feet, seeking to offer her own brand of support. Eventually, I was calm again. "Thank you," I said in a whisper. "I'm sorry to be such a wuss."

He huffed a laugh I could feel, warming and somehow reassuring. "Not a wuss, Maggie North." He drew back enough to mop my eyes with a paper napkin. "An idiot sometimes, but never a—oof!" He grunted when I pushed my elbow into his ribs.

"As Trilby would say, with his advanced vocabulary," I said primly, "it takes one to know one. You're a lawyer, Eldridge—how could you possibly call someone else an idiot?"

"Well, though, you know, I'm not a very *good* lawyer. I've never even been on TV. I mean, I've been on camera walking out of the courthouse with my shirt coming untucked and my tie loose because it was choking me, but no one in the media ever chases me down and tells me I'm brilliant." He looked thoughtful. "Kind of pisses me off."

"I don't blame you. That's upsetting."

Then we were both laughing. Chloe went back to guarding Ezekiel, undoubtedly relieved she'd saved her person from certain meltdown destruction. I stepped away from Sam, but he pulled me back to him, and we shared some of the kind of kisses that often lead to satisfying interludes.

"Come on," he said.

I looked up into his face, startled. "Come on where?"

"Let's play some music. Jim Croce's in my head today."

"But we still have pizza, and I want more wine."

He went back and refilled my glass, got another beer from the fridge, and gestured toward the pizza. "Bring it with you. I'm yearnin' for some Leroy Brown."

"Fine." I picked up my plate and followed him to the alcove at the end of the living room. I put the pizza on the end of the piano bench and set about limbering up my fingers. I hadn't played in church that morning, claiming pain in my hands—not mentioning that it was in my heart, too—and apologizing profusely. One of the summer women had played instead, expressing regret for not being prepared.

There was a lot of apologizing that morning, which Cari mentioned, and then she told us if the sermon bored anyone, that was just too bad—she wasn't *about* to say she was sorry. So, the service had ended up being lighthearted and hopeful, two things there'd been a real need for— from my side of the lake anyway.

We played for an hour and a half. We got through my limited repertoire of Croce classics in the first twenty minutes, but I was so charmed by them that we played them all again. By the time I played "Morning Has Broken" all the way through without stopping, my hands were screaming at me.

I stopped, looking at Sam where he sat with the Guild in his hands. He'd known what I needed even more than I had myself. The fact that I'd been able to replace the words Greg had erased from my computer had been a big step through the mental and emotional morass created by his presence; playing music with hands he'd thought he'd damaged beyond repair had been another. Taking care of little Ezekiel was yet a third.

Look to the sun, Margaret Mary. That's where you'll find it.

I wasn't sure what I was looking for, but Trilby's words had stayed with me since the day I first read them. I could do this. With the help of my friends, I could do it.

~*~*~

I stood outside on Wednesday morning while Chloe took her constitutional to the edge of the woods, looking around. I wasn't scared this morning, but I wasn't comfortable, either, especially when I saw the hummingbird feeder lying in pieces at the foot of the shepherd's hook where it had hung since Uncle Bill brought it home from the flea market. Beside the red glass pieces lay the candle holder from the bistro table on the deck. It had undoubtedly been the weapon used to break the feeder; it wouldn't have shattered if it had fallen to the grass on its own.

Mental abuse isn't the same as physical and emotional, but it's a deeply personal violation nonetheless. I shuddered and looked up and around again, hoping he was gone.

"Chloe?" I spoke sharply, and she gave me a questioning look before ignoring me and going on about her business. "Come, Chloe."

She obeyed, reluctantly, and we went back into the house. I locked the door and reset the alarm. "We better hope we never have a fire," I mumbled. "We'll never make it out, and if we do, we'll step on glass left behind by a narcissistic whack job."

The dachshund looked worried, and I bent to pick her up, stroking her silky ears. "We'll be fine, but you better work on your ankle-biting skills. They might be needed."

After calling the sheriff's office to report the vandalism, I went back into the office, carrying a big enough insulated cup of coffee to get me through until hunger laid claim to my attention.

The writing of *Mayhem on Monday* had gone fast, regardless of my attempts to slow down and enjoy the story. I hadn't looked ahead by so much as a paragraph since I'd started, and nearing its end, I still didn't know who the killer was, where the sapphires were, or—quite literally—who they belonged to.

Legends, I explained to Chloe and Ezekiel, are supposed to be clear-cut, with well-defined edges to them like retention ponds. The story of the sapphires, on the other hand, was more like Harper Loch. Its edges slipped off into inlets and coves that made for good fishing but sometimes difficult mowing. While some of the stones had come from a foreign land, there'd been no secret to it—they were the wedding jewelry of the woman who'd come to America with her new husband. Others had been added as their family and their fortunes grew. They were bought for love and beauty more than value, and sometime late in the twentieth century, interest waned.

The legend itself had been embellished into what was likely a far grander story than the real one. The fortune itself—at least in the book—was considerable by my standards, but I can't say how it would have been ranked in upper echelons.

I would be surprised if anyone outside of family members or very close friends would recognize Trilby's oblique references to them or their histories. I expected most of the purchases and sales hadn't occurred the way they were described, yet the basics rang true. Trilby's notes were more emotional than usual, even including allusions to faith. Readers had always been aware that Finlay Iverson was a backsliding Presbyterian and that his best friend from the very first book through the last, Darby Pierce, had once been a minister, but they were never made privy to his actual beliefs.

If I worked hard today, as I intended to do, I would reach the end of the book. I would know the answers.

It was, at the end of the writing day, somewhat different from the previous Mayhem books had been. Other than straightening its timeline and getting rid of anachronisms, I hadn't changed much at all. I'd typed most of the notes verbatim, filling in spaces with Trilby's writing voice. The book was a few thousand words shorter than usual and its subplot—only one in this volume—was more succinct.

As I'd feared and at some level known, Finlay Iverson died in this story. He had found the killer and the sapphires, the story twisting at very nearly the last minute in ways that would surprise all but the most deductive of readers. In the final few pages, we discovered that the headaches Finlay first developed in *Mayhem at Howard's* were indeed indicative of a massive stroke in the offing. With his final case solved, he went to bed and never woke up. It had been Trilby's intent, so I wrote it that way.

I have no words to fully explain how much I hated it.

I emailed the last chapter to Miki to see what she thought, copying the email to Ellie, Trilby's sons, and my aunt and uncle…even to Cari, along with a note apologizing for blowing off another Wednesday coffee. Crying hard enough that Choe climbed into my lap and licked my chin, I sent it to Sam, too. He'd gone back to Muskegon on Monday, leaving me strangely bereft even though I'd told him I needed time to myself.

It was late. I didn't expect to hear from anyone until the following day. I left the office, turning off its lights and closing the door. I carried Ezekiel's basket into my bedroom, Chloe following along. She took her responsibility as the kitten's caregiver seriously.

I went to bed, double-checking the alarm system and carrying my wineglass. The dog and her kitten were sleeping. I changed into clean faded pajama pants and a tank top and washed my face, noting that my eyes looked as if I'd been awake for days … possibly weeks.

When I turned off the bathroom lights, a shard of brightness flickered on the round window, and I turned them on again. I wasn't sure if car lights from Enoch Trace would bounce off that window or not, but it made me uneasy.

Was Greg out there? Waiting. Watching. Was he, like the killer in his brother's last book, searching for the sapphires?

I stared at the window. At the decorative piecrust edging around its circle of panes. None of the leaded glass windows were exactly alike, and I knew they'd all been created and put into place by local artisans—including Annabelle Newland. Some were more perfect than others, although I think it would take a glazier to understand why.

Suddenly, inexplicably, given how exhausted I was, I knew where I'd seen the window design before.

I knew.

But I didn't know why.

Chapter 17

I didn't act on what I'd figured out. The time would come when I'd need to, but I was a great respecter of the *just a feeling* that suggested I wait. While I'm sure I'm not naturally intuitive, being intimately acquainted with both Trilby Winterroad and his alter ego, Finlay Iverson, I've learned to catch things that slip into the periphery of my thoughts.

Tom and Dan sent a joint response on Thursday afternoon. "Painful, but wonderfully written. Probably Pop's choice."

"It's wonderful," said Miki over the phone forty-five minutes later. "Maybe some of the best writing you've ever done. You had me in tears."

"I feel betrayed," said Ellie flatly. "I have no explanation for that, but it's how I feel." She'd read it on her phone during her lunch hour, but waited until after work to call.

"I'm withholding judgment," said Cari in a return email. "I'd like to talk about this, but only if you want to."

"Are you all right?" Aunt Lin sounded cautious, and I understood why. Better than anyone, she knew how much I'd already lost. Writing Finlay Iverson's death had been like losing Trilby all over again. "Not that it isn't good, but … I just need to know you're all right."

Sam didn't answer his email, but when I was constructing a salad the size of a small city that night, the bell at the corner of the Burl rang. "You look like hell," he said kindly, when I opened the door. He held up a bag from a deli he and I both loved. "How about dinner?"

"Don't you ever have to work?" I closed the door behind him. "Thanks for the sandwich, though. Want some salad? By the way, no woman likes to be told she looks like hell." I caught sight of myself, reflected in the window over the sink. It was not an improvement over the night before after finishing the book. Had I even combed my hair today? Or brushed my teeth? "Great Santa's beard, even if she does look exactly like hell—especially if she does."

Sam put the deli sandwiches on paper plates, cut them in half, and set them on the placemats on the counter. "You want some coffee?"

I shook my head, setting down wooden bowls of salad. "Tea." I'd drunk so much coffee lately that the idea of one more cup made my stomach hurt. "Did you read it?"

"I did." He moved around the kitchen as if he'd been here a hundred times, which he may have.

"How many words this week?" he asked.

I laughed, understanding his reference to my half-penny-a-word bonus, and noticed he hadn't said anything about the final chapter.

"The book came in at seventy-eight thousand words," I said, "and I wrote almost half of them this week."

It wasn't the first time I'd done that. One of the Lunchroom Mysteries had been on a wicked deadline and I'd written the whole thing one spring break when Trilby and Claire took their entire family to France for ten days. It was invigorating, writing that fast, but it was exhausting, too. I'd taken off the entire month of May after finishing that one and learned to play the ukulele.

Sam had been in the ukulele class, too, and we used to go out for a beer afterward. At the Winterroads' Christmas party, we played and sang "Mele Kalikimaka."

"We were never invited to perform again," said Sam, getting up to pour boiling water into the teapot.

I stared at his back, lean and straight-shouldered in a flannel shirt that shouldn't have looked professional but did. "How did you know what I was thinking?"

"I didn't." He set the pot in the middle of the counter, then got a mug and spoon out for me. "But I did remember the other time you wrote that fast. Claire was mad at Trilby for letting you do it."

“I needed to.” It had been the year Greg went to prison. I wasn’t afraid anymore, but I also didn’t want to see anyone or be near anyone other than the ones I considered family. They’d suffered enough for my idiocy.

But Sam had dragged me off to the art gallery where the ukulele class was. So much of that time was a blur that I wasn’t surprised I’d forgotten that.

“Thank you,” I said.

“For what?”

“The ukulele class.”

“We were awful.”

I nodded agreement. “But it was two hours a week that nothing hurt except my fingers. I lived on pain pills and that one beer a week there for a while.”

I’d been so terrified of addiction that Trilby had kept track of the white capsules as long as I took them. At the same time, I was so repelled by even the thought of touch that I don’t think I touched anyone for months after leaving the hospital with my body mostly healed and my heart and mind a mess. I wasn’t a toucher anyway, so to speak, but I’d avoided it altogether, wearing braces on my hands in public even when I didn’t need them anymore because no one expected me to shake hands as long as I had them on.

I’d come a long way since those days. I shook hands freely now, especially at church, and sometimes the late-day walkers held onto each other's arms. I exchanged hugs with Ellie and more than that with Sam. Touch had become a welcome thing without me even noticing it.

Could I still be that way, or had I lost it when I wrote the last chapter of *Mayhem on Monday*?

For reasons I couldn't explain, my thoughts segued to Finlay Iverson, to him bellowing *great Santa's beard!* when he really wanted to cut loose with a string of curses. He'd been such a complete persona, and his readers went to every place in his life with him.

No wonder Ellie felt betrayed. No wonder I felt as if I'd lost myself.

I'd finished my sandwich without realizing it, and was sorry to see my empty plate. How long had it been since I'd eaten? I drew my bowl of salad toward me.

"He wouldn't have given up, would he?" Not that dying from a massive stroke was in any way giving up, but I understood that Trilby hadn't considered his own death giving up, either. He hadn't wanted those he loved to suffer through his final days. Controlling to the end, he didn't want to suffer himself, either.

Do I know that for sure? I kind of think I do. It's the only way to make sense of how he died. He'd lost weight before he died, and energy along with it, but he never admitted illness, just *I'm old, that's all.*

Sam's smile crooked to the left. "Finlay? I don't think so, but you and Trilby knew him better than I did."

He was right. We had. And I knew him better than Trilby. In the last chapter of the last book, I'd ended his life as Trilby had stipulated, but it wasn't right. Not for Finlay or for the Mayhem readers. Or for me.

Find your own voice.

"I have to rewrite the last chapter."

Sam smiled, the expression reaching and lightening his eyes. "I think that's a wonderful idea."

I spent several days on the last chapter this time, getting back into tune with a still-healthy Finlay and enjoying the dry humor his creator had given him. I had to work hard to keep it consistent. Relief at my favorite sleuth living to snoop another day was giving me the tendency to overdo it.

I hoped Trilby wasn't shaking his fist at me from somewhere for going against what I knew he'd wanted me to do, but Finlay deserved better. His readers deserved better. *I* deserved better.

Truthfully, I felt as if we'd deserved better from Trilby, too, but that hadn't been my decision to make. I hadn't been able to rewrite how he'd chosen to end his own story.

"I'm so relieved," said Aunt Lin over the phone, when I told her I was rewriting it.

"Me, too." And I was. The door wasn't closed on the Mayhem books, although I didn't know that anything would ever come of it being left ajar. While I had some courtesy say on what happened with the brand, the final decision—at least through the end of this book—belonged with Trilby's family.

Tom and Dan's return emails after reading the new chapter said the same thing: *Yes! Yes! Yes!*

Only Miki sounded doubtful. ARE YOU SURE? Her text sounded anxious, and she called before I had a chance to answer it.

"I'm sure," I said into the phone without preamble. "New readers of the series wouldn't like knowing the hero ends up dying down the road."

"You're right," she said instantly. "And on a strictly professional basis, I'm glad you changed it. Personally, though, I want it to be okay for you. I had the feeling you were following what Trilby wanted."

"I was." A part of me felt as if I'd betrayed Trilby by going against what his sons and I all knew had been his wishes; however, I really, really liked the idea of that door being left open a crack and they did, too.

Find your own voice.

I had, and I'd used it.

"I think Trilby would be okay with this," I said more firmly than I felt.

"Then I most certainly am." I could hear the relief in her voice.

Approval among the readers of the new chapter was consensual, except that I hadn't heard from Sam. I knew he was busy. Much of his work had to do with elder care, and sometimes it got ugly. It wasn't different, that we didn't keep consistent contact, but it *felt* different because we'd become closer since he'd first driven over to the lake. And I liked it. I liked it a lot.

My phone chimed a text message, and I looked at the screen. There were two symbols there. A red heart and a thumbs-up. From Sam.

Cari's "Son of a Preacher Man" ring tone sounded from my phone. "I'm an idiot," I said by way of greeting.

"Well, I'm glad you said *I* instead of *you*," said Cari, "although you wouldn't have been the first one to have said it. What are you talking about? Do you need me to do a pastoral intervention? I'm sure I'd be great at it."

I burst into laughter, making Chloe sit up and look at me. "Not yet, although I'm sure it's coming. Did you need me for something?" I kind of hoped she did—I thought my brain was fried.

Was that yet another cliché?

"Actually, I wondered if you'd like to go to Squirrel Creek. I have a friend from culinary school coming for dinner soon and I'd like to impress him."

I loved Squirrel Creek. "Sure," I said. "I need some flour anyway. Want me to drive?" I knew she would—Cari hated to drive.

"I thought you'd never ask. I'll come there, though. The road guys are working on Enoch Trace on this side of the lake and you can hardly get around. Half an hour?"

"I'll be ready." Which meant getting dressed. I looked regretfully at my computer screen, where I was clarifying things in the last chapter. I was leaving as much in as I could from Trilby's outline and the notes, although they'd become more cryptic at the end of the book. I wondered what he'd been trying to tell me. I still didn't know, and I wondered if I was overreacting to my unilateral decision to change the ending of the book.

I saved changes and closed the file. I'd think about it later.

Fifteen minutes later, dressed in my favorite capris and a black sleeveless top, with my hair captured into a ponytail, I took Chloe out, peering around the back yard for any sign of activity. Nothing had happened in the days since the broken hummingbird feeder several days before. Other than a few walks around the lake with the late-day walkers, I hadn't been anywhere because I was exhausted by the writing marathon. For hours at a time, I'd stopped waiting for the proverbial other shoe to drop.

I frowned at where my car sat on a concrete pad beside the driveway where Sam said Harp had parked a motor home. I hadn't minded parking outside until lately, when it seemed to become an open invitation to vandalism. If Greg knew how much I liked my little blue car, it probably would have already happened.

"Chloe!" I called sharply as she made a beeline for the woods. She stopped, but didn't head back in my direction. She stood beside a clump of purple iris that had volunteered and faced me, not moving from the spot. "Come on," I called.

She didn't.

Annoyed, I stepped off the deck. "I have to go, Chloe—Cari will be here any minute. You've just cost yourself a treat, and when I tell your favorite babysitter you've been a bad girl, she'll be mad at you, too."

I stopped in my tracks. Was I really talking to a dog like she was a child? I was just one step away from babytalk. Even Trilby hadn't done that, although I'd heard him process plot points with her. He'd insisted she was very helpful.

Chloe's whimper recaptured my attention, and I hurried on toward her, wondering if she was hurt. "What's the matter, girl? You didn't see a porcupine, did you?" I picked her up, searching for injuries, then started back toward the house.

As I reached for the handle of the back door, I felt something … or maybe smelled it. I wasn't sure which. I couldn't hear or see anything other than my car across the driveway, but something was off. Finlay Iverson would be lifting his head in search of the reason. *Something's in the air*. I'd typed it at least once in every book. What I hadn't written was the full-body shudder that accompanied the sensation, the suggestion of nausea at the back of my throat.

Chloe barked sharply, twice.

With only that much warning, my pretty blue car exploded before my eyes. Although occurrences like this seemed louder in movies, I didn't remember ever hearing the shattering of glass the way I did with the inferno across the drive. It wasn't nearly as neat, either. Shrapnel hit the driveway, even coming as far as the deck where I stood transfixed by the scene before me. The deep, shiny blue paint that had made me buy my car untested off the lot disappeared in the firestorm ignited by what almost certainly had to have been a bomb.

Still holding Chloe, I backed into the house when flames leapt toward the trees that lined the driveway, calling 911. I was abstractedly grateful my phone was set up so it took just one urgent tap on the screen to make the connection.

“They’re on their way,” said the dispatcher tersely. “Please find safety.”

I didn’t know how to do that. I’d already come into the house. Was it safe or were there more bombs there? Would the toilet blow up if I had to pee? Would I—

Cari!

I set Choe down on a chair and let myself out the front door, terrified of what I might see. The car had been some distance from the house, but the fire had been a huge, terrifying mushroom.

A message sounded from my phone, but I didn’t take time to look. I had to make sure Cari was all right. What if she’d been coming up the driveway when the car had ignited? What if … was Greg really that crazy?

What was I thinking? Of course he was.

Alarms seemed to be coming from everywhere, although I knew there was only one road that led back to the lake. The sheriff’s SUV pulled in and to the side so that it wouldn’t be in the way of the fire engine with its distinctive air horn and wailing siren.

Running right up the middle of the driveway was the pastor of Harper Loch Community Church. She was safe. Safe. And now she was going to get run over if she didn’t get out of the way of the emergency vehicles converging on the Burl.

I yelled, “Cari!” and took the porch steps two at a time. I ran across the lawn faster than I thought I had in me, trying to get her attention over the cacophony of sounds. "Cari! I'm all right!"

The relief on her face when she saw me would bring tears to my eyes when I thought about it later. At the moment, though, I just wanted to get us both out of the line of traffic.

Even as the fire engine drew closer, Sam's truck came from the other way on Enoch Trace, moving much faster than was either safe or legal. He pulled into the driveway, the back of the pickup fishtailing, and drove into the yard. I had the abstract thought that he'd run over his mother's peonies. The black vehicle stopped with a jerk beside where Cari and I stood together, and he jumped out, leaving the truck door open and the engine running, and pulled me closer than I'd been held since Tim North died.

"You're all right," he said. "Oh, God, you're all right." Without letting go of me, he hooked an arm around his niece and kissed the top of her head. "How did you beat me here?"

"I was supposed to be here. We were going to Squirrel Creek." Cari mopped at her eyes with his shirttail. "But Maggie set her car on fire because she didn't want to drive."

I laughed, although I was still shaking all over.

"Chloe?" said Sam, just as her sharp bark made itself heard from inside the house. "Oh, good."

The scene, which seemed to go on for hours, became surreal. Although no one got in the way of the emergency vehicles, virtually everyone I knew on Harper Loch arrived within minutes. The front yard, so neatly kept by Jake and Emily, filled with cars, golf carts, and bicycles.

"We are quite literally ambulance chasers," Colby admitted, "but we are always grateful when there's not an actual reason for the ambulance."

The sheriff approached, his face set in grim lines. "You spoke too soon, Colby." He nodded in my direction. "Ma'am, if you could come with me?"

With Sam on one side and Cari on the other and Colby following behind, I accompanied the sheriff to the other side of the driveway. Haley Squires, who I knew to be a trained EMT, was kneeling beside what appeared to be a body.

I stopped, dread feeling like molten heat; I knew it couldn't be running through my veins, but that's what it felt like. "I don't want—"

"Just to identify," said the sheriff quietly. "He won't hurt you now."

Sam drew me to his side, keeping his arm around me.

My feet felt like lead, but we followed the sheriff.

Time in prison hadn't been kind to Greg Mathis. The hair that had been thinning when I knew him was gone now, although I thought he probably shaved it, since he didn't have the slightest of horseshoes of hair around the sides of his head. He'd gained weight in the wrong places and his once-handsome features looked somehow fallen. Had I met him on the street, healthy and on his feet, I'm not sure I would have recognized him.

"Maggie." My name whispered from between his lips. "Didn't want to hurt you."

The words startled me. Good God, what would he have done if he *had* wanted to?

"I waited … waited … till you went to get the dog to detonate." He chuckled, a macabre, whistling sound. "Must be slowing down…I didn't get away in time."

I couldn't tell where he was hurt. There was a lot of blood, and his face was devoid of color.

"Sorry to have … hurt you." Speaking was obviously an effort. "I always meant to … be a good guy …l ike the Iverson dude. Just never worked out. I wanted the sapphires, was all. Trilby didn't need them anymore."

"Okay." I didn't know what else to say, so I said it again. "Okay."

His eyes widened, and Cari dropped to her knees beside him, taking one of his hands in hers. "Dear heavenly Father of mercies …"

I closed my eyes, not praying, but respecting Cari's calling to do so. When I opened them again, Greg Mathis was dead.

Chapter 18

The ringing of the bell at the corner of the house made me stop obsessing about my hair and leave the bathroom. "Hey, Flynn," I said, opening the door to the mail carrier. "Baby?"

"Not yet," he sighed. "Amy says she's not really pregnant—she just inadvertently swallowed an acorn and she has an oak tree growing in there."

I made sympathetic sounds. I knew the baby was four weeks from its due date and Amy was miserable.

"I have a registered parcel that needs your signature." Flynn looked apologetic. "It's ashes."

"Oh." I looked at the orange sticker on the Priority Mail box that identified its contents. CREMATED REMAINS. "Oh, well. Okay." I signed the handheld device and set the box on the counter. "Give Amy a hug for me," I instructed, handing Flynn a bottle of water and a recycled cottage cheese container full of cookies.

"I would," he said morosely, "but I can't get my arms around her anymore."

"Have you mentioned that to her?"

"Oh, hell, no."

We parted laughing, and I got a cup of coffee and stood looking at the box. I'd known it was coming, but now that it had, I didn't know what to do with it. With him.

He hadn't been religious and I hadn't really considered he had a soul, but Cari had prayed for its salvation anyway. I hadn't done any forgiving yet. I wasn't at all sure I ever would.

Coffee was at the Burl that Wednesday the ashes arrived. When we were gathered, cups of preferred beverages in hand, instead of sitting down at the table in the alcove, we all stood around the breakfast counter and looked at the box.

I said all that I'd been thinking since Flynn brought the parcel. "I don't know what to do with them."

"You could put them in the cemetery," suggested Rose. She grinned a little wickedly. "No one there would mind."

"The lake." Sadie nodded wisely. "We could assign it to the writer kids to write about. I'll bet they could create some mind-boggling scenes."

"Nightmare scenes," you mean, said Dallas, trying to keep a straight face and failing so miserably that we all ended up leaning on each other, unable to stop laughing. She had the kind of laugh that you couldn't resist unless there was something seriously wrong with you. Or even if there was, because I was feeling particularly afflicted as well as conflicted today and I still laughed until my stomach hurt.

Emily shrugged. "If you just want to put them in the woods, it's a peaceful place."

Haley spoke. "When the boys' dad died, we'd been divorced for a long time, longer than you had, but the ashes still came to the house—Flynn had to deliver them. Paul had never married again, so it fell to Flynn and Eamon to decide." She smiled across the counter at her daughter-in-law. "Remember, Amy?"

"I do."

"What did you do?" I asked.

"The boys got to talking, remembering things from when they were younger, when things were … different. *Do you remember?* they would say, and they talked about their dad coaching them in baseball. I was the team mom and Eamon was the bat boy. Flynn played first base. It was about the best time in our lives all together." She stopped for a moment, as if remembering. A smile curved her lips and her eyes were damp. "It was about midnight, I think, and we all piled into my car, including Amy, and drove to the park in Placer. The boys spread ashes all the way up the third base line."

I remembered that I couldn't forgive myself for how stupid I'd been to have fallen for every promise, every joke, every shared sunset that built my relationship with Greg Mathis. After we separated, Trilby advised me quietly to "let go of the good," and I had done precisely that. I still wasn't very forgiving of myself, but it did release me from the *what should I have done differently?* mire I'd freefallen into.

I was glad Haley and her boys had held onto enough of the good to have done the perfect thing. I just wished I could come up with something that would leave peace in its wake.

We talked about flowers then, about summer plans, about who'd bought the cottage beside the Bee, about Eamon being accepted at Northern Michigan.

Only Cari was quiet, and when the others left, she stayed, stirring her coffee and staring at the box of ashes. I refilled my own cup and sat across from her, waiting. I was prepared for the conversation we were about to have. At least I thought I was.

She set her spoon down on the cloth napkin, then picked up her cup. And set it down, the coffee untasted.

When she met my eyes, it was as if she had to force herself to do it, and I smiled at her, hoping to be encouraging. "Cari?"

She nodded, and looked away … gathering her thoughts, probably … then looked back.

"He asked me to do it," she said. "The Winterroads and the Newlands were best friends all the time I was growing up and we were present in each other's lives. Claire's touch with French cookery made me want to go to culinary school, Grannabelle taught me about stained glass and making quilts, and Grandpap taught me to fish." She laughed, although moisture had crept into her eyes. "When I was drawn to ministry and followed the call kicking and screaming all the way, Trilby taught me how to write and deliver a sermon so that people might at least occasionally listen to what I was saying."

"He taught you well, but you had the heart and the words to make it work." It was how he had taught me, too. Except that while I could write and deliver, most of the words and heart had been his.

Cari nodded. "He told me that part was up to me."

I could almost hear him saying it.

In the book I'd just finished, there were obscure references I hadn't been able to pin down. It had made it hard to tie up loose ends, and the rewriting of the final chapter had meant retying those ends. Even now, when I thought I knew most of the answers, there were a few that still gnawed at me.

Cari spoke again. "He'd never asked anything of me, you know. Even when I went to see him the week he died because something had felt wrong in our last phone conversation, he didn't…" Her voice trailed off, and when she spoke again, it was tremulous. "He didn't let me know what his plans were, although I understood from what he did say that he was dying. He gave me the sapphires and asked me to put them in the window here at the Burl. He told me which window, so that you'd catch on when the sun shone through. He thought it would be easy for me to disassemble because I would know how it went together."

Look to the sun, Margaret Mary.

"I have felt the most tremendous guilt. My sister says it's because our family has so many religions and all of them are built on feminine guilt. I didn't argue with her because I'm not entirely convinced she's wrong." Cari looked away again. "But I couldn't do it, in the end. Not that I didn't want to, but I'm not a good enough glazier to do it without risking the stones."

At first, I was surprised, but then I wasn't. I'd been taking things far too literally—not the first time I'd done that. "He knew, didn't he? That you didn't want to risk it."

She nodded. "He came up with the alternative plan, but I still felt bad that I couldn't do what he wanted. I did what he asked, though. I know where they—"

That's where you'll find it. For better or worse.

So that was it. But instead of replacing the first clue in his note, he'd added another that changed things altogether.

I held up a hand to interrupt her, so sure I had the answer that I was almost giddy with it. "I think I know, too. You can go with me, to tell me if I'm warm or cold." I got up, heading toward my bedroom.

She didn't say anything, but she followed; I think she knew this piece of something unknown was Trilby's gift to me. Leaving the door open in case Chloe came looking for me, I turned on the lights and went to the end of the bed, looking down at the sunburst on the lid of the dower chest. I frowned at the contents, seeing nothing, then began to lift them out. An extra set of sheets, although I always put the same ones back on; the quilt I took off the bed when I put on the new one Aunt Lin made; an extra feather pillow she'd re-ticked when she was here. I stacked them in the wing chair I sat in to read sometimes, then lifted out Tim's shaving kit. I'd brought it to the lake with me, afraid to have it travel in the truck with the other things I'd shipped.

It was full of things. Notes we'd written to each other, his last driver's license, his sunglasses, his wedding ring, the memory card from his funeral, more than I could remember as I sat and held the zippered case. Sometimes, just to be able to draw those memories close, I would open the kit to touch the things inside it, but it had been a long time since I'd needed that. I stroked a hand over the leather, thinking for a couple of heartbeats that maybe … but, no … she wouldn't have known.

I had to stop for a minute. To breathe. "A dower chest is like a hope chest," I explained. "I never had one, and you probably didn't, either, but my mother did. Yours might have. They filled them with things to take into their marriages." I don't know why I thought I had to explain it.

Cari nodded. "My mother did."

Setting the shaving kit aside, I lifted out embroidered pillowcases and dresser scarves I hadn't known were there and a soft merino shawl I recognized as having belonged to Claire. Another wooden box sat on the faded shelf paper that covered the bottom of the chest. "A handkerchief box," I said. "Aunt Lin has one from her mother."

"This one was Claire's." Cari's voice caught. "She brought it from France."

Ah. I hadn't been exactly right. I'd thought there would be a secret compartment in the bottom of the chest, and maybe there was, but I didn't have to look any further.

I opened the box.

The stones were beautiful. Some of them were in old fashioned settings, large enough they looked ostentatious to me—making me think again of the cocktail rings in Trilby's books. They'd been mentioned in the last one, too, one of the dated references that made me blink. None of these pieces of jewelry were that ornate, but I couldn't imagine wearing them. One of the rings was a duplicate of the wedding ring Greg had given me, although the stones in the cache I spilled onto a cloth on the Burl's kitchen counter looked clearer. Prettier.

A manila envelope had lain beneath the velvet pouches of jewelry and loose gems in Claire's handkerchief box, folded carefully in half so it would fit. My name was written on the outside in Trilby's distinctive hand.

Cari stopped me when I started to open it. "I'm going home. I think this is between you and Trilby." She hesitated. "I'm sorry I didn't tell you. I couldn't. Trilby wanted you to figure it out on your own." She smiled, although there was anxiety in the expression. "He said you were always the first one to solve the Mayhem mysteries, that he never let you know what was going on until you figured it out."

I nodded. "That's exactly the way it was, too. I understand why you waited." And I did. I was glad she'd honored Trilby's wishes as well as she could. I hugged her, holding her closer than I normally would. "No guilt, okay?"

When she'd left, I checked on Ezekiel, who was already being cared for by his adoptive sister, and went into the bathroom to gaze at the window Cari had created. I was glad the sapphires weren't there, because I loved the little window exactly how it was. Cari hadn't known me when she created it, but I felt as if she had.

Back in the kitchen, I poured a glass of wine and sat at the counter to peel open the self-seal on the envelope. Most of the papers were copies of documents certifying some of the gemstones. There was a photograph of Claire and Trilby in Paris when they were young, the Eiffel Tower holding place of pride in the background. Claire was wearing a pendant, the only piece in the collection I really liked, and they were looking into each other's eyes.

Another envelope was at the bottom of the stack of papers. Like the large brown one, this little one had my name on it, too. It was the kind of stationery Claire used to have. Onionskin thin, but soft lavender in color, with her name and the address of the farm in purple in the center of the envelope flap.

The writing on the sheet of paper inside the envelope was Trilby's, and it was from the legal pads he and I always used at the office. His were always yellow, but mine never were. The memory made me smile.

Margaret Mary:

If you're reading this, you've solved the mystery, haven't you? You know there's no real legend to the sapphires, only that Claire and I collected them because we liked them. We bought the pendant she's wearing in the picture on our honeymoon.

At one time, some of them came up missing after a visit from Greg. It didn't take long to find out he had stolen them and subsequently sold most of them. Your wedding ring was made from the smaller, cheaper ones. He didn't think I would recognize them, but I didn't write Mayhem books for nothing—I learned a lot in the process.

If we'd had a daughter, Maggie, we'd have wanted her to be you—although Lin and Bill had already staked that claim. At the end of Claire's and my lives, we want you to have the sapphires. Do what you want with them. Claire thought you should open a bake shop and make cinnamon rolls for a living. I think you should invest them in something important to you and write books. Ones from your heart.

I imagine you've finished the book by now. It was a hard one, put together from the past and from both wishes and mistakes made. I hope you change the ending. I hope you forgive me for writing it the way I did.

Well, thank goodness that's over.

Love, Claire and Trilby

Instead of putting the stones back in the dower chest in my room, I stored them and their documentation in the safe in the office. Not that I was worried about them—it just seemed like the thing to do. I kept out the pendant Claire had been wearing and put it into the envelope with Trilby's letter and the picture.

The house was silent. I couldn't even hear the wind chimes on the back deck. I felt lonelier than I had in a long time. I wished my aunt and uncle were here, or that Cari had stayed, or that it was the night the writers' group came. I longed for Tim, to feel the way I'd felt then. I even longed for how much I'd liked being alone before I came to the lake. That certainly wasn't the same anymore.

I wished for Sam.

The late-day walkers texted as I sat there. I almost ignored the series of messages, with their ringtone of Patsy Cline's voice singing the first four words of "Walkin' After Midnight," then shook my head at my own sad vagary; hadn't I just been indulging in a pity party about being lonely?

Doors in my life had closed today, but as the old saying promises, windows had opened. I looked at the box of ashes I'd moved to one side when I sat down with the sapphires and the envelope. *Tomorrow. I'll decide tomorrow.*

Scarlett O'Hara and I had it going on.

There were ten of us that night, all women. A few drove together from Placer to join us. Several of them had been at coffee that morning. We entertained each other by explaining why we were or were not wearing the same clothes we'd worn then.

The night was warm, the air soft. I looked at them as we walked and talked. I listened to their stories—

Trilby taught me a lot about listening and its importance.

We've all known struggles and heartbreak; several of us have known physical abuse. Sadie had lived in her car for a while when she got a divorce. Rose had left Colby in Detroit and come to the lake, saying he could come or go; it was up to him. Adrian told the story of her Uncle Henry's father beating his wife half to death because their son "wasn't right."

Maxine said her husband had raised his hand to her exactly one time and she told him he'd better not let it fall or he'd never, ever be able to go to sleep again. We laughed at that, but she didn't. "I was scared to death and so was he. Not that I'd kill him, but that he'd gotten so angry over something minor. He got himself to an anger management therapist and I went along with him. But I'm aware every day that we're the lucky ones. Our lives could have gone a whole different way from that day forward than what it did."

We've laughed together at the images people have of others' lives. While Harper Loch doesn't look anything like a resort or even a high point on rural Michigan's social scale, it does look like a place where bad things can't happen. Where marriages are all good, no one uses illegal substances, and everyone is safe.

But we know better—and it's not lost on me how often I use the word *we* when I talk about the lake.

We've absorbed each other's pain. I didn't know how Cari could bear the weight of the secrets she kept.

"How many women around here have been abused? Not just on the lake, but in the area."

"More than we know," Rose acknowledged. "Just like anywhere. Some talk about it, but more than a few don't."

"Many," Haley agreed. "Because they think it's their fault or it's never going to happen again or they don't have any alternatives."

I thought of those women. Of their children. I thought of the people who'd circled the proverbial wagons around me to keep me safe. I thought of Cari and Ellie and the confidences they kept and carried with them. I thought of Aunt Lin and Claire and Annabelle and how strong they'd been when their lives turned on them.

I thought of the ashes. And of the sapphires.

Chapter 19

I think maybe Greg loved his biological mother. His father was never part of the picture, but he lived with his mother when he wasn't in foster homes. She was an addict, but she used to visit him and tell him someday they'd be together. One day early in our marriage, we had a picnic and then we went to the cemetery where she was buried. Her grave had one of those temporary markers on it. He said he'd like to buy her a granite one, so we did.

"I'll take the ashes there," I decided. "If he cared about anyone, it was her." I think he loved his adoptive parents, too, but he'd never felt like he belonged to them. He'd always resented that Trilby was not only the elder, but their biological child as well.

I was in Muskegon for a few days, visiting Ellie and Jax and transferring my banking to the branch in Placer. The permanency of that felt strange but right.

While I was there, I visited a couple of women's shelters and talked to the people who ran them, to a few others who'd once needed shelter and were now giving back, to a child who wasn't scared anymore. I didn't ask anyone's name and no one gave me one. I left donations and felt helpless and hopeful at the same time.

I'd left spreading Greg's ashes until last, either out of dread or because I wasn't absolutely sure I was doing the right thing.

"I'll take you to the cemetery," said Sam, when I stopped by his office to drop off some paperwork. "We can look at some cars while we're out, but we'll go in my truck."

It made him crazy that I hadn't replaced my car yet. The rental I was driving was … okay. It was white and boring, but I just couldn't care about that right now. "Maybe," I said, but I didn't mean it.

I had to look up the cemetery where Greg's birth mother was buried, only remembering that it had the word *peace* in its name. It was about fifteen miles outside of Muskegon, but it felt farther because it was an area I'd never had any reason to go. The gravesite wasn't very well taken care of, nor had it been before, but I found the stone easily.

Sam opened the box and pushed the bubble wrap within it aside to bring out the sealed plastic bag that held the ashes. "Do you want me to do it?"

I did, but I shook my head anyway. This was on me. I spread them slowly enough that I hoped I appeared respectful and repeated a prayer I'd heard Cari say the day he died. I stood silent then, not knowing even now what I should do to close the door on that episode. Should there have been a funeral? I'd thought of it, and Cari said she'd officiate if I wanted to have one and Trilby's family said they'd attend if I needed them to, but in the end, I couldn't face it.

Sam's arms came around me from behind. He didn't say anything, either, just held me until I drew myself up straight and said, "Let's go."

I asked him to drive me past Tim's and my dream house when we got back to town. He parked across the street from it, and I got out of the truck, crossing to walk past it slowly. The new owners had replaced the sidewalk with one made from used brick—it was nice. I hoped I didn't look like a stalker, but I needed to say goodbye to the dream Tim and I had shared.

I didn't need it anymore. The Burl had taken its spot. I thought of the man in the truck and spoke softly to the man I had loved before him … still loved … not caring that I would look like I was talking to myself right out in public.

"I'll always miss you," I whispered. "You're the love of my life, but you'd be happy with me and for me now, I think."

It might have been my imagination, but I didn't think so. The breeze, which had been nowhere to be found all day, brushed against my cheek, loosening guitar-string wiry hair from its loose braid. I will always believe, not because I need to, but just because I do, that it was my love kissing me goodbye.

I sauntered back to Sam's truck, feeling more at peace than I had since … I don't know when. My tall lawyer friend with the beautiful gray hair and the cerulean eyes that spoke to me without words came around the front of the pickup and opened the passenger door. He put a hand on my elbow to help me into the tall vehicle. I could do it myself, but it wasn't pretty when I did.

Besides, I liked the sensation of his hand on my arm.

I turned instead of climbing into the truck, so that I faced him, my hands resting on his chest. He released my elbow so his arm could come around my waist and draw me close enough that his legs and his flat stomach were against mine. I could feel his strength and I enjoyed it, but mostly I was just conscious of him being there. Exactly where I wanted him to be.

"Tim North was the love of my life," I said, even now missing him. It didn't hurt anymore … not really; rather it was part of the knowledge that we'd been so lucky, he and I, to have found each other and shared our lives.

"I know," said Sam. "He was one of the best people I've ever known. Other than his unfortunate penchant for winning video games, that is."

"He was always admiring of your *fortunate* penchant for losing them, too," I remembered. I nodded in the direction of the little house across the street. "It used to be red. That was one of the things we loved about it—that and the fact that we could almost afford it. I was thinking I might paint the shed at the lake red and have a little porch built on the front of it. Just big enough for a few chairs and a swing."

"Sounds like a good idea. We can get some paint before we go back today. I used to paint houses in the summer while I was in college. I'd paint during the day and umpire Little League at night. I had a lot more energy then."

"I remember. You painted Claire and Trilby's farmhouse one year."

"Tom and Dan and I did," he corrected. "What were you thinking of doing with the shed?"

I was a little shy about my plans, although I was surprisingly unafraid he wouldn't like them. "You spend so much time at the lake now, I thought maybe you'd like to have an office there."

Something kindled in his eyes. "That would be nice."

"I've realized something."

Two teenagers passed on bicycles. I expected jeers of the *get a room* variety, but they just waved and rode on. They made me think of the young writers at the lake, and I smiled. I loved those kids.

"What?" said Sam.

I looked up. "What what?"

"What have you realized?"

"Oh." I edged even closer and smoothed the placket of his shirt. I unfastened the top button, then pushed it back through the buttonhole. "That sometimes love just happens without you even knowing it. Like how I feel about Jax and Cari and the writer kids. And the people at the lake who've made me so welcome that the Burl has become my home to the extent that I can never imagine living anywhere else."

Sam nodded. He raised a hand and pushed my hair back where it was falling out of its braid. It was always in my face, even when I tried to keep it up or back. Why couldn't I have been a good-hair person, one with pretty hands and eyes that didn't look like old denim?

"I feel at home at the lake, too," he said. "I really like the idea of having a satellite office in the shed. I like how much I see you."

He caught my right hand and looked at it, turning my wedding ring from Tim around and around.

"I promised him." My voice was raspy, and I cleared my throat. It didn't help. "I promised Tim that I'd put it on my right hand when I made room for someone else in my heart. I didn't think I ever really would, you know? But that day when the car exploded and I saw your face when you got out of the truck, I knew I had. I knew that, *voila*, a girl can have two loves of her life."

He was silent for a moment—not long enough for me to shrink into humiliation, but I withdrew a little. Had I spoken too soon? Had I seen and felt things that weren't there?

But then his hands curved around my face and he was kissing me. It wasn't sexual, exactly, although there wasn't a doubt in my mind that it could become that way. We had examined that part of our relationship, and quite successfully at that, but it had been done with longing and mutual respect and … I think, feeling safe with each other.

Standing inside the cove created by the half-open door of his truck, heedless of Sycamore Lane's light traffic and the bicycling teenagers who rode past again, riding either with one hand or no hands as they ate ice cream cones, the kisses we shared were more. They were a promise, the safe place so maligned in politics by those who thought they didn't need such things.

They were, I knew when we finally stoppcd to takc deep breaths and rub noses and laugh a little shakily, a declaration.

Both Miki and the publisher were happy with *Mayhem on Monday*. There would be revisions—there were always revisions—and for the first time, discussion of the cover design would be up to me instead of Trilby. It was too bad he hadn't left me a note with clues about how to take care of *that.*

In the same conversation, I talked to Miki about writing under my own name. I wanted to try historical romance. When she told me to go for it, I sent her an email that said *The heroine's name is Annabelle. The hero is Harper, but everyone calls him Harp. Annabelle is the pastor at a community church in the woods beside a lake. Harp owns the bait shop and is no longer a believer. A gust of wind takes the steeple right off the church and lands it in the bait shop parking lot.*

She told me to send the first three chapters and the synopsis and she'd see what she could do. Since I just happened to have those ready, I sent them by return email on the last Monday in June. She kept the chapters, but sent the synopsis back early Wednesday morning with comments and suggestions that doubled the length of the document. I gawked at it on my computer screen, closed the file, and left the room. What had made me think I could actually write a book someone else hadn't outlined for me? I texted her, maybe sounding a little testy. WHAT DO YOU THINK OF THE CHAPTERS?

I LOVE EVERY SINGLE WORD.

Oh, okay.

HOW'S SAM DOING? I MISS DEALING WITH HIM. HE'S ONE OF THE FEW LAWYERS I'VE KNOWN WHO DOESN'T TREAT ME LIKE AN IDIOT.

THEY ONLY DO THAT SO YOU'LL TRY TO GET MORE MONEY IN CONTRACTS.

SO, YOU DON'T WANT TO TALK ABOUT SAM?

I felt heat climbing my cheeks. I would be fifty-three at summer's end, and I still blushed like an eight-grader. And I called her—sometimes texting was just stupid. "He's here. Actually, he's in his office." She didn't know it was in the backyard and that he wasn't *in* it; he and Jake and a few of the fishermen were busy drinking beer and building the porch on the imaginatively named RED SHED, SAM ELDRIDGE, ATTORNEY AT LAW.

I left for Wednesday coffee as soon as I hung up, thinking when I approached the parsonage that today was a repeat of the first day I'd gone except that instead of snow falling, it was eighty-nine degrees and humid. It was hot enough I would have driven, but I hadn't gotten a new car yet, regardless of Sam's urging and our visits to every dealership between Placer and Muskegon.

We all got there at the same time, although I didn't see how Amy Squires could still walk. The number of us varied from week to week, but today we were a dozen.

"I've been thinking," I said. "I talked to Tom and Dan about the sapphires. I said if they or Miriam and Josie wanted them, they could have them. As I knew they would, they said no. So I said I'd like to sell them and use the money toward opening a women's shelter because there isn't one nearby. They wrote me checks. So, what do you think?"

"I think," said Rose slowly, "that when we have the Fourth of July picnic, we should ask for donations to the cause."

"Picnic?" I said. It was the first I'd heard it mentioned.

"Why, yes," said Emily. "It's an annual thing."

"Where does it take place?" My question met with silence and I looked up to see the others exchanging looks. "Did I say something wrong?"

"Not wrong," said Sadie slowly, "but we thought you might like to have it at the Burl. The garage is huge and so is your yard."

"We can haul the tables and chairs over from the church," Cari offered. "If we keep the main course to hamburgers, hot dogs, and bratwurst, everyone else will fill in all the sides."

"How many years has this picnic been going on?" It seemed odd to me that I'd never heard anything about it and the Fourth was only a week away.

"Counting this year," said Rose, "it will be one."

Once the seed was planted, the First Annual Harper Loch Fourth of July Picnic—yes, every word of that went on the poster that appeared like magic that very evening at the church, the mercantile, and Lavender Park—became a thing to the entire eighty-six. At least, it seemed that way. Lawns weren't a big deal at the lake. Although we—or in many cases Emily and Jake—kept them mowed, and many of us had a lot of flowers, trimming was haphazard, and there wasn't a manicured yard on the whole lake. Even Lark Meadow's neatly terraced front lawn had its shaggy spots.

Jake rented a pull-behind finish mower and mowed the deep grass between the lake and Enoch Trace. One of the residents of the second row was so impressed, he paid for an extra day with the mower and mowed at the sides of the back road. Several of them even went together and put up a street sign proclaiming the recently widened lane to be SECOND ROW.

We set up the food in the garage. Some of the guys dragged in a few pallets from behind the mercantile and nailed together a makeshift bar over by where the overflow refrigerator sat. They filled the fridge with beer and bottled water. Ellie borrowed a 12 -bottle wine fridge from the Black Dog and brought it along with a couple of bottles of something far better than Scott ever sold.

After I made sure to invite Mr. Henry and Adrian from the convenience store to the picnic, they came out to the lake and he set bud vases Cari brought from the church on every single table, then put wooden roses into each vase. I didn't cry, no, not me. Neither did anyone else who was there helping set up. Our eyes always look like that.

Sam went to Muskegon on Monday to meet with a client and pick up some local beer. When he came back that night, he wasn't alone. Jax was in the passenger seat, the cases that held his drum kit secured in the bed of the truck. A one-year-newer replica of my beloved blue SUV pulled in behind them, driven by my forever car guy, Uncle Bill. Aunt Lin got out, waving eagerly, and I burst into tears. I wasn't even denying them this time.

After everyone finished hugging everyone else, I pointed at the car. "What's this?"

Sam's arm came around my shoulders and I leaned into him. "The dealership called and said they'd just found this. They were the clients I needed to meet with. It's not a done deal—if you don't like it, we'll take it back."

"You'll love it, guaranteed," said Uncle Bill. "I buried her speedometer on the way here and she didn't even sneeze." He grinned, tugging at my ponytail. "Of course, your Aunt Lin smacked me a good one, but it was worth it."

The picnic was everything we could have hoped for, and more. Even looking back on it and trying to count, I have no idea how many attended. The food was the embodiment of the loaves and fishes parable. Every time Uncle Bill, Sam, and Colby took the last meat off the grills, someone appeared beside them with a foil-covered cookie sheet filled with squashed and seasoned burgers, bacon-wrapped hot dogs, or parboiled bratwurst. Every possible recipe for potato salad, slaw, and pasta salad was represented in bowls on the food tables. Cari offered grace in her very best preacher voice, and we ate and talked and laughed all afternoon.

Everyone watched the little ones in the wading pool someone brought and filled with the hose, especially Amy, who was near enough to her due date that everyone on the lake was on pins and needles waiting for her to yell, "Now!" and go immediately into hard labor. Flynn sat with her, reaching periodically to rub her back. Sometimes they sat with their heads together, and he would make her laugh.

Claire's handkerchief box, labeled with an imaginative sign saying SHELTER DONATIONS, was filled with everything from collections of pennies to checks that made my eyes widen. I put the contents in the safe and set the box out again.

Sam and I were apart most of the day, both of us working to make this party the success we wanted for Harper Loch and the eighty-six. And for the women's shelter that would be Trilby's legacy.

People played horseshoes, cornhole, and volleyball until tiredness began to set in in early evening. Then Jax set his drums up on the concrete pad where my car had burned that fateful day in May and not only Sam's guitar came out, but others as well. A few harmonicas slipped out of shirt pockets. Sadie brought a flute from its case. Haley Squires, wearing a beautiful floaty dress, swept the bow lightly over the strings of a violin she held, and I swear, the whole group of us went, "Ahhh…."

I went inside to replenish the lemonade and tea coolers and when I came out, Jax was setting up an electronic keyboard. "The keys are all there," he promised when I gave him an accusing look. "I counted 'em."

"Does your bandmate know you took this?" I asked in my best pretend-mom voice.

"Sure, he does. He's hoping you'll lend it a little class by playing it."

He set a tips jar on a lawn chair in front of where the musicians played, propping another SHELTER DONATIONS sign in front of it.

We played until almost dark, songs from every decade any of us could remember, and then played some more. My fingers were fixing to fall off by the time Jax broke a drumstick and Sam broke a string on the same song and we knew it was time.

The crowd dispersed slowly, many of them still singing as they went. Their voices were haunting as they floated back toward us when they walked or drove away down the Trace.

I had to stop Aunt Lin, Miriam, and Josie from digging into the cleanup. "It will be there tomorrow," I said. "Jax and Sam are taking care of the musical instruments and everything else can wait. Let's just make some coffee and take that last pie out of hiding and relax over them before we go to bed,"

"Good thinking," said Miriam. She looked over at where Tom and Dan were folding chairs. "I really hate to stop them from working."

"One more thing!" Sam called out. "Cari, come back here. We'll take you home, but I have something to say first. Come on, Jax. This is a family thing."

We all met at one of the cleared tables. Although Trilby's grandkids weren't here, his sons and daughters-in-law were, Jax was, Cari was, Ellie, Aunt Lin and Uncle Bill … it did indeed feel like family.

Sam got down on one knee.

There was a collective gasp.

"Who's going to help you up from there?" I asked, because I was suddenly nervous, and a shared laugh followed the gasp.

"You are," he said simply, "because that is what we are to each other. That and a great deal more. We love each other, you and I, and we've been friends ever since Trilby brought us together all those years ago. He kept us together with the Burl and that fishing shack at the end of the lake. He loved us both, just as these people here, do, and we loved him, just as we do this pieced-together family of ours."

He took my hands in his. There was no desperation in the touch, no grasping, just warmth and tenderness and … oh, yes, and promise, too.

"I know we said we weren't worried about being married, that it was enough that we were just having a great time together, but we were wrong, Maggie North. Tim wouldn't be at all happy about us having any kind of refusal to commit and you know it as well as I do. I want to spend my life with you if you'll have me. Will you marry me? Oh, and Wilbur. You and Chloe and Ezekiel have to take him, too, because I'm moving to the lake."

Our gazes met and clung, and it was like dancing. I loved him so much. "Yes," I said. "But you and Wilbur will have to be patient with Chloe. She'll share me happily, but Uncle Bill is all hers."

"That works for me." Sam reached into his shirt pocket and brought out a little box. "It's not a diamond," he said quietly, "but I thought it suited you. If I was wrong, we can take it back. It's not part of any legend or collection—it's just for the story of you and me."

The sparkling sapphire sat between two small diamonds on the white gold band, winking and promising in the outside light. "It's perfect," I said, just above a whisper, and held my left hand out for him to slip it on my finger. I had no doubt it would fit, and it did. “Let me help you up so I can kiss you.”

“All right.” Still holding my hands, but not really needing my help, he got to his feet, kissed me pretty thoroughly, then turned to where my aunt and uncle stood together. “Do we have your blessing?”

Perfect. The man was perfect.

“You do,” said Uncle Bill solemnly. “Are we correct in assuming free legal consultation comes along with the marriage? Not that it’s a deal-breaker, but just sayin’.”

“Bill!” Aunt Lin smacked him, then kissed him, then drew Sam and me both into her arms.

I don’t know what time it was when we began drifting into the house. I didn’t have to do anything else. They all knew where their rooms were. There were towels in the bathrooms, new bars of soap, candles, and updated magazines.

Sam got up. “I’m taking Cari home,” he said, “and then I’m going to spend the night in the fish shack.”

“You don’t have to do that,” I said. “Aunt Lin knows I’m not a virgin anymore.”

Cari gasped. “You’re not?”

We laughed again, and shared a three-way hug.

“I think, my beloved, you’re ready for some quiet. While this new social butterfly I’m going to marry is purely delightful, I also know inside her there's the quiet loner I fell in love with who needs to be alone with herself sometimes."

I couldn't deny it. "See you in the morning?"

"Eventually. Bill and I are taking Jax fishing and then to the mercantile to lie about what we caught. The boy needs to know these things." He kissed me, that sweet loving meeting of our lips and hearts that I would never get enough of. "Goodnight, love."

I got a bottle of water and went into my office, not even looking for Chloe—she was with my uncle. Ezekiel was curled up on the chest in front of the office windows. I closed the door behind me and sat at the desk. I was so very tired, yet so enlivened by the day this had been, by the ring on my left hand, by being in love with both Sam and this place I lived. I wasn't ready for bed.

My book, the first one I'd be writing with my own voice, my own heart, waited for me. I could almost hear Trilby's voice. *Well, Maggie, are you ready?*

The thought made me smile.

I looked at Tim's picture on my desk several pages later, and turned the worn wedding band round and round on my right ring finger. It was more snug on my right hand than it had been on my left. I would probably take it off someday, but not yet. "I wish you were here, love. I wish you knew I was going to be all right."

I remembered that breeze a few weeks ago. I closed my eyes and rested my hand on my cheek to recapture the sensation it had brought.

He knew.

Epilogue

Amy's water broke on the way home from the picnic, and Bridget Haley Squires was born a few minutes before midnight on the Fourth of July. Haley was beside herself. Aunt Lin spent the entire day of July fifth in the quilt room making a blanket for the new baby.

Two weeks later, little Bridgie was wrapped in the blanket when she was christened in front of most of the eighty-seven other residents of Harper Loch. The church was too crowded to have coffee and donuts afterward, so we all went to the Burl and had them. Amy and Flynn had asked that no one bring gifts because certain family members and friends had already bought their daughter more than she'd ever be able to wear or play with. Everyone agreed and brought money instead. Except for Jax, who bought her a drum.

While we were there in the backyard at the Burl, Sam and I went ahead and got married. I was wearing a dress, after all, and Aunt Lin and Uncle Bill were flying home the next day. Ellie was there for the weekend, so she stood up with me and Jax stood with Sam. After the ceremony, one of the writer kids read Civil War soldier Sullivan Ballou's letter to his wife Sarah. Haley, who'd brought her violin to play a lullaby at Bridget's christening, played "Ashokan Farewell."

I hardly cried at all.

That evening, preparing dinner in the Burl's wonderful kitchen with Aunt Lin, I thought of everything that had changed since Trilby's death. I still missed him. It hadn't been long enough for me to have come to terms with his death, but I'd come to understand it. When I thought of how he'd engineered my life to give his plans and wishes for me every chance of succeeding, I had to laugh, although I'd have resented that level of interference if he were still living.

I couldn't take exception to it now, though. He'd been right. Again.

The colors in the transom drew my eyes as I rinsed pasta in the sink. I loved the blue—I always would—but I appreciated the value of the other colors now. Just as I cherished being alone, I had learned to thrive in the company of others. Music wasn't solitary anymore, and life was seldom quiet. While I would never have kids of my own, I had ones to love. I would never be a grandmother, but Haley would share Bridget with me.

Behind me, Chloe yipped and Wilbur hissed something rude. "You two get over yourselves," I said, bending to stroke them both, and they trotted off together, Ezekiel hurrying along in their wake.

Sam stood at the doorway into the kitchen, smiling at me. When I stretched out my hand, he took it and we went out through the mudroom to the deck. The wind chimes, made from bells, lent music to the evening breeze. And we danced.

The End

About the Author

She wanted to shake the dust of central Indiana farm country and move to the city, get rich, wear designer clothes, and write books.

Well, she writes books.

Liz Flaherty lives five miles from where she grew up, only now she relishes the sights and sounds and scents of the fields around her, doesn't care much about clothes, and thinks being rich would probably have been overrated anyway. She's spent the past several years enjoying not working a day job, making terrible crafts, and writing stories in which the people aren't young, brilliant, or even beautiful. She's decided (and has to re-decide nearly every day) that the definition of success is having a good time.

Along with her husband of lo, these many years, kids, grands, friends, and the occasional cat, she's doing just that.

Please find and join her at her website: https://lizflaherty.net and on Facebook: http://www.facebook.com/lizkflaherty

www.ingramcontent.com/pod-product-compliance
Lightning Source LLC
LaVergne TN
LVHW010642110826
845149LV00014B/2922

* 9 7 8 0 9 9 7 1 6 3 7 6 6 *